Amba Yahaluwo

T. B. Ilangaratne

Translated by
Seneviratne B. Aludeniya
from the original Sinhala Novel
Amba Yahaluwo

sarasavi Publishers
No.30, Stanley Thilakaratne Mawatha, Nugegoda.

First	Print	1998	
Second	Print	2000	
Third	Print	2003	February
Fourth	Print	2003	July
Fifth	Print	2004	June
Sixth	Print	2005	January
Seventh	Print	2005	December
Eighth	Print	2006	October
Ninth	Print	2007	May
Tenth	Print	2008	September

ISBN 955-573-058-X

Cover by Priyanjan Suresh de Silva
(Photo courtesy : Ashain Manjula)

Printed By
Darshana Marketing Enterprises (Pvt) Ltd.
107, Kaduwela Road,
Battaramulla.

Preface

After reading Mr T. B. Ilangaratne's Sinhala Novel "Amba Yahaluwo" I enjoyed it so much that I conceived a desire to translate it into English for the English reading public.

Even after a considerable lapse of time I am now happy that I was able to fulfil my desire. But if I had been able to translate it while Mr Ilangaratne was living I would certainly have been happier then than now.

I thank my sister, Mrs Tamara Kumari Ilangaratne for helping me to obtain permission to translate the book into English, and also for attending to matters regarding the publication of the book itself.

Seneviratne B. Aludeniya

66/46 Devana Rajasinghe Mawatha
Kandy
18. 02. 1998

Other Books by the Author

Sinhala Novels

Amba Yahaluwo	Nedeyo	Kelemal
Sasara	Nivena Ginna	Malsarawa
Lasanda	Peraliya	Sedapahara
Hetak Nethi Lowak	Priyadaraya	Vilasithavo
Dayadaya	Ambalama	Yovun Viman
Himi Gamanak Gosin	Okkoma Rajavaru	Sethapuma
Nodaruwo saha Daruwo	Aiyala Nangila	Hapana
Thilaka	Thilaka ha Thilaka	Delova Sihina
Nayana	Mangala	Lokanthaya
Vilambeetha	Darusurathal	Diyaniya
Mangala Poruwa		

Children's Books (Sinhala)

Pissu Lucy	Aluth Malli	Thaththa
Nimalage Upan Dinaya	Tikiri saha Kuda	Tiger

Drama

Jathaka Natya	Rangamadala	Heramitiya
Manthri Hamuduruwo	Handahana	Nataka Ata
Sakunthala	Nikan Ava	Sailasanaya

Short Stories

Onchillawa	Ranmenika

English Novels

Match Maker   Inseparables (Original Translation of
Amba Yahaluwo)

Translations

Denuwara Kathawa (Translation of " A Tale of Two Cities")

Autobiography

Yugayaka Gamana

Chapter one

Nimal came running past the other boys and leapt from the road on to the grass and picked up a mango.

" That's mine " said Sunil trying to snatch it from him

" I'll give you ! "

" How could the mango I picked up be yours ? "

" May be you picked it, but I am the one who saw it first. "

The other boys walked about under the mango tree looking for mangoes. A few boys picked up good ones, some even picked up mangoes partly eaten by squirrels while some were deceived by immature ones that looked ripe.

Sunil who only wanted to get the mango Nimal had picked up got nothing.

" Are you giving my mango or not ?" asked Sunil and rushed towards Nimal leaving the satchel on the ground and fought for the mango.

Nimal too thrust his bundle of books under his armpit and held the mango with both his hands. Because of the quarrel the books slipped and fell on the ground. The other boys who picked up mangoes shared them together.

" If you want a piece I'll give you one" said Nimal still fighting.

" Why only a piece for me?"

The fight increased in intensity. Both of them fought rolling on the ground, crawling on their knees and by getting up and falling several times over. The other boys who were only interested in enjoying the taste of mangoes thought that it was a mock fight at first and made fun of it. But when they saw the angry faces of the fighters they were drawn towards the scene of the fight.

" What's this? " asked one.

" He is trying to take the mango I picked up " said Nimal without giving up the mango.

" I am the one who saw it first, " said Sunil drawing his fist and giving Nimal a powerful blow on the forehead.

Nimal who did not expect this blow was thrown aside and it was with difficulty that he prevented himself from falling on the ground. The boys were alarmed. Without trembling Nimal continued to look at Sunil silently. Sunil also stood up preparing to hit him if the need arose. Immediately Nimal stepped forward and offered the crushed mango to Sunil. Sunil drew his foot back and kicked Nimal's extended hand. The mango slipped out of his hand and fell on a rotten mango covered by a swarm of blue flies. Still Nimal kept on looking at Sunil. Sunil too stared at Nimal like a fighting cock.

" In vain! None got it " said some boys. Nimal wiped the mango juice that soiled his hands on his trouser pockets, dusted his clothes and collected his books when a fully ripe golden mango fell in front of Nimal and he picked it up.

" See how the squirrels selected the correct side, " said Nimal. Sunil who heard it looked up as if he intended to hit the squirrel.

Nimal took out his penknife from his pocket, opened it and

cut the mango. The boys surrounded him. Nimal pinned the first piece of mango with the tip of his knife and offered it to Sunil. Sunil looked at Nimal's face and as he saw it tears gathered in Sunil's eyes.

" Take Sunil, take " said one boy. Sunil looked at the piece of mango and Nimal's two innocent eyes twice or thrice, then he turned back, picked up the satchel and went away.

Chapter two

Sunil was ten years old and younger to Nimal by one year. Nimal was so strong that he could have beaten up Sunil. But Nimal did not beat him. Therefore Sunil felt sorry. With down-cast eyes and full of thought he went away along the road.

How bad it was for him to have kicked Nimal. Nimal did not even speak. How cruel was Sunil not to have taken the piece of mango. Sunil felt shy. The other thing is to whom did the mango belong ? Sunil might have seen it earlier. Whoever saw it first, doesn't the mango belong to the person who picked it up ?

The clock at the Moratu kade, near the bridge, struck two. Sunil stood there and looked back. Still the clique of boys did not come. The boys were students of the fifth standard at the Nelumpura Gemunu Vidyalaya. They lived in the same cluster of houses in the village. In the morning Sunil went in the car with his father. When school closed at one thirty in the after-noon it was his habit to join the other children and go home together walking. However when they come up to a distance from where they could see the mango tree they run and pick mangoes.

Almost every day it was Nimal who ran and got under the mango tree first. It was mostly for this that Sunil got angry with Nimal. But what a cruel thing Sunil did ! He was unable to pardon himself for doing this.

" Patience begets relief " was written on a school plaque which Sunil remembered. He realized the truth of it that day without any effort. Nimal will of course, like the other boys, sit under the mango tree for a little while and come. Just like the other boys he'll be crying out " O squirrel, O squirrel give us a mango to eat " at this time. As a reward for his patience Nimal should have received immediate relief. But Sunil on the other hand decided not to do that kind of thing ever again.

Had he hurt Nimal? Had he sprained his arm? Had mango juice soiled his clothes?

Sunil who saw the clique of boys coming at a distance resumed his journey.

On the sleeve of Sunil's crumpled white shirt there was a patch of mud. The blue pair of shorts too was dirty. Since it was Friday it did not matter; because on Monday he would wear a new suit. The black pair of shoes was covered with dust. Sunil saw this and standing on one leg he wiped his shoes with the Grey socks. His slightly curly hair which was parted on the left was a little dishevelled. His broad forehead was smeared with sweat mixed with dust. And as a reason of the warmth of the sun and the effect of the quarrel his slightly dark cheeks looked flushed and bright. Since his mouth had struck Nimal's knee his upper lip too was slightly swollen. As a reason of all this Sunil's mischievous appearance showed itself more prominently than his good looks.

It was Sunil who had good clean clothes than all the others in the group He did not wear any suit for more than two days. That may be the reason why the other boys treated him with particular esteem. The lady teacher had a faint fondness for him. This made him worried at times. He also felt shy. He thought how good it would be if he also could be like the other boys. Yet he sometimes took pride in being treated with a particular regard by the other boys.

Whatever it was how crude was the manner in which Sunil behaved under the mango tree. If Nimal too treated him in this manner what would he have done?

Nimal wore only a pair of brown canvas shoes. After the quarrel Sunil saw that one of Nimal's shoes was smeared with cow dung. What a pity! Sunil heard Nimal saying once that he has only three pairs of blue shorts and three khaki shirts. They were worn after being mostly hand washed at home. As a result of the quarrel Nimal's shirt would have become dirty. What was he going to wear on Monday? Of course towards the end of last month Sunil's father had brought home six suits stitched on one occasion.

If Nimal had hit him at least one blow he would not have been hurt so much. Was Nimal a coward ? It cannot be. He remembered one day that a boy in the sixth standard was given a good beating. Yet why did not Nimal speak a word against Sunil who kicked him?

Paddy fields on either side of the road were ripe. Sunil bent down towards the field and plucked an ear of paddy. He bit off paddy grains one by one and ate them after removing the husks as he went along. It may be that since the sun was not so bright paddy birds in flocks flew hither and thither early. A parrot too flew towards the clearing adjoining the paddy fields carrying an ear of paddy. The tin hat of the scarecrow in the centre of the paddy field shone in the sunlight.

Sunil left the stretches of paddy fields and walked close to the stone quarry.

" Sudu Appo, alone today?" asked the quarry man taking his straw hat in his hand. He was a sturdy man wearing a pair of native shorts. He placed the hammer on the ground and stood erect. The bare upper part of his body was bathed in sweat. He curved his right forefinger and wiped the sweat off his heavily scarred broad forehead. Sunil had seen him standing in his courtyard several times; not in this dress but in a sarong and gauze banian. Therefore he was not able to recognize him at once.

Sunil smiled at him picking up a stone threw it into the stream below. A rabbit which was on the bank of the stream being frightened at the noise scuttled off wildly through the scrub jungle.

" Where is our boy, Sudu Appo? "

" Who is it? "

" Nimal "

" There he is coming "

" Why didn't he come along with you, Sudu Appo? "

" Nimal has got angry with me " said Sunil picking another stone and throwing it in to the stream.

Presently Nimal emerged from the curve of the quarry alone. The other boys had turned at the junction near the bridge and taken the other road. Sunil and Nimal came as far as the stone quarry. Nimal walks down from the quarry. From there onwards Sunil goes alone.

The quarry man broke off a stick from a nearby Hinguru bush. "Why didn't you come with Sudu Appo?" asked the quarry man from Nimal in a stern voice raising the stick. Nimal looked into the distance without talking. " Have you got pittu in your mouth?" yelled out the quarry man. He hit him once and said,

" Haven't I told you to come with Sudu Appo?" and raised his stick again. Sunil rushed in and held the stick which was in the quarry man's hand.

" Don't hit Nimal " said Sunil. The quarry man's face lit up with an unusual smile.

" Because of Appo I have tolerated you today, if not I would have skinned you " he said by way of rebuke and threw the stick away. " Appo loves you so much, why can't you come with him because he comes alone. Run home, have your meals and come with your sister to break stones " said the quarry man. Nimal walked down from a spot close to the quarry and disappeared.

" Can Sudu Appo walk this distance alone?" asked the quarry man.

" Yes "

" Otherwise am I also to come?"

" Don't " said Sunil and walked away thoughtfully

Chapter Three

Sunil's house stood on the upper side of the road. It was called Aluth Walauwa. Sunil climbed the three rows of steps leading to the courtyard of the house thoughtfully.

" Mother?"

" Yes, son"

" Are you asleep?"

" No "

Sunil kept his satchel of books on a table and went towards the dining table. The mother got rid of her drowsiness and having gone towards the dining table removed the reed cover and served the food to Sunil.

Sunil's mother is Nelum Kumarihami. She was about thirty years, fair complexioned, tall and slender. She was wearing a blue saree and a white blouse. " Queen Elizabeth is just like mother " is what Sunil often said

" Are all your sums correct, son?"

" Yes, don't serve me bitter gourd. What's this?"

" Wetakolu "

" That too, I don't want "

" Then here are beans "

" That too, ha ha a little "

" Dry fish? "

" One piece: what meat is that? "

" It's straw mushrooms Don't you want? "

" I want; I want a little more "

" This is mutton "

" A little "

Sunil began eating.

" Start mixing the rice from one end, son "

" I forgot "

" Yes, you always forget "

" Why, didn't I eat well last night ? "

" Eating well once is not enough, you must eat well every day"

" Will it be late tonight too when sister comes, mother? "

" No, appachchi said he will come early today "

Nelum Bandara is Sunil's appachchi. He is the chief clerk at the courts. He goes to office in the car. When he goes he takes Sunil and his sister Maithri. This is because the time of the courts tally to a great extent with that of her school. But since Gemunu Vidyalaya closes at one thirty in the afternoon Sunil comes back walking. Sunil ate his food thoughtfully.

" Mother, who is that man who breaks stones?" asked Sunil finally .

" Which, with the beard?"

" No, the other one "

" Who has a scar on his forehead? "

" Yes, yes ".

" That man is called Galbanda ", said Nelum Kumarihami and smiled humorously.

But Sunil put on a serious look.

" Not that! I mean the name in the book "

" In what book? " The mother suppressed a smile.

" The true name? "

" That man's true name is Muthumale Walauwe Muthu Banda; after he came to that house he was called Galwalegedera Muthu Banda. For convenience all called him Galbanda "

" What a pity "

" Why do you ask ? "

" Just "

" Why just "

" Please mother shall I go to break stones? "

" Why? "

" No, I love it so much "

" Why is that ? "

" A boy in our class too will come to that quarry to break stones "

" A boy in your class? " asked the Kumarihami amazed.

" Who is he? "

" Nimal; he is Galbanda's son "

" Is he also in putha's class? "

" Yes, why? "

" Aney, Aney " said the Kumarihami in surprise.

" What is it? " asked the grandmother coming towards them. She is the mother of Sunil's appachchi. The older Kumarihami is good looking, well groomed and buxom. Her face is round and she is fat. He hair is silver grey and her face is wrinkled.

The mother was still smiling.

" What is it daughter? " asked the grandmother

" Nothing. Galbanda's son is said to be in putha's class"

" Is it true? " asked the grandmother surprised.

" Do you know what his name is? It's Nimal " said the mother smiling again.

" This is the curse of teaching them free; and all the riff- raff going to big schools, " said the grandmother with force.

" Don't you go even to talk with that sort of fellow " she advised Sunil.

" Why grandmother? "

" There, you question me. I say don't because it is no good"

" Listen a little to what I say will you " said the grandmother as if she were a little angry.

The conversation mixed with humour that took place between the mother and the grandmother was not understood by Sunil. Sunil who started thinking about it did not even care about what he ate.

" Son why do you eat only curries? " asked the mother and once again started serving him curries.

Chapter Four

Since it was Friday there was no need for Sunil to change his clothes. The mother had given him permission to wear at home the clothes that he had worn to school on Friday.

After he had eaten his lunch he took his shoes off, patted the dog Neela which was tied in a corner of the building where the barn was and went under the lovi tree in the courtyard. He did not go there for any special reason but happened to go there without any conscious effort. He only thought of Nimal. Sunil could not forget him.

Sunil stepped down into the garden of the walauwa. There were two grown trees, a betel creeper climbing a Kahata tree, a Cashew tree with an earthenware pot in which there were honey bees and a sweet waraka tree. He passed them all and went down. He then came up to the fence and reached the sour guava scrub jungle. The sour guava fruits were ripe. He hastily plucked a few and ate them. They were sweet like bee's honey. He crammed his two trouser pockets with guavas. Then he put guavas right round the waist between his body and the shirt.

Sunil then remembered the story of Columbus. Columbus sailed the seas and discovered a new land. Can't one go on land and discover a new land? Sunil went further into the land. A mongoose ran away in front of him. The crickets which were deceived by the darkness of the woodland began screeching. Sunil fearlessly went further. A wild mango had fallen on the ground. He picked it up and gnawed at it. It was sweet. It could be said that it was even sweeter than the kind known as papaw mangoes. There were three more. He picked them up too and went further down. On a tall guava tree there were three fruits. Sunil climbed it and picked all three of them. He remembered princess Madri who went to pick fruits in the jungles. Is it difficult to live only on fruits. Sunil sat on a bough of the guava tree and ate some of the guavas. He then heard a voice; It was somewhat familiar to him. Yet he was unable to identify it at once.

" Mother why is it that we don't have rice today too? " asked the familiar voice of a child.

" Although we had broken stones we did not get money for it yet", answered an unfamiliar female voice. Sunil looked around. He saw a shanty at the foot of the slope. The conversation came from that direction,

" Why, the paddy of this field? "

" This does not belong to us "

" Why? "

" We have sold this "

" To whom? "

" To Aluth Walauwa "

" Why is that? "

" Your father got entangled in a land case and as he could not pay the lawyer's fees he sold the paddy field "

" To whom? "

" To Aluth Walauwa "

" Then Sunil and the other's will be having rice every day "

" Who is Sunil? "

" He is in our class, that's the boy from Aluth Walauwa. "

" Is Sudu Appo's name Sunil? "

Sunil's doubts were cleared.

That was Nimal and his mother.

" Even to make roti why did you take such a long time. mother? " asked Nimal.

" I came only now after plucking tea leaves "

" Where did sister go? "

" She went to Ihalagedera to pound rice "

" Then sister will be bringing a little rice? "

" Yes "

Sunil got down from the guava tree and proceeded towards the hut. The hut was thatched with coconut leaf. The walls were of wattle and daub and the floor was smeared with cow dung.

Sunil walked towards the front of the shanty.

Nimal clad in sarong and a banian was seated on a bench. He was holding an enamel plate on his left palm and eating roti with scraped coconut. Nimal who heard footsteps looked over his shoulder and after keeping the plate on the ground got up.

" Sunil, where are you going?"

" I came for a walk "

Instantly a woman came out of the house. He also heard the babble of little children. Sunil became aware that they too were eating roti.

" I was wondering who it is; it's Sudu Appo isn't it? "

" Where are you going this way? " asked Nimal's mother.

Sunil easily recognized Ranmenika. He remembered that she came often to Aluth Walauwa to pound paddy. She was clad in a soiled jacket and a chintz cloth with red flowers. Nimal's mother resembled him very closely.

" I just came " said Sunil bashfully

" In this jungle? " she asked and smiled.

" Come Sunil, sit down " invited Nimal.

" Call him Sudu Appo son, otherwise they will blame us " said Ranmenika.

" It doesn't matter " said Sunil going inside the house.

" It's a pity! There isn't even a place for Appo to sit down ", she said and spread a piece of paper on the dirty bench.

Sunil sat down after putting the paper aside.

A voice was heard calling " son, son ". That was the voice of Galbanda.

" Why appachchi? " Nimal went out and shouted back.

" Are you coming or not to break stones today? "

" Son tell him that we are coming ", said Ranmenika. It could have been heard by Galbanda, too.

" Are you coming to break stones today or tomorrow?" asked Galbanda as if in anger.

" Then we'll go " said Sunil

Sunil and Nimal went off towards the stone quarry. The two friends crossed the stream. Until then they did not talk much. At last Sunil broke the silence.

" Nimal, are you angry with me? " asked Sunil holding his hands and looking at his face.

" No "

" I feel very sad because I hit you "

" That doesn't matter "

" Did your arm hurt you? " asked Sunil rubbing the back of Nimal's palm.

" No it didn't hurt me " said Nimal although the hand was slightly swollen as a result of the kick with the shoe on.

" You even got a beating from your appachchi because of me isn't it? "

" It doesn't matter "

" I will never hit you again " said Sunil taking the finest guavas and the mangoes from his pocket and offering them to Nimal.

Nimal took a few of them.

" Where are you going now Sudu Appo ?"

" Chi! Don't call me Sudu Appo ; call me Sunil just as on other days "

" If appachchi hears, he'll beat me "

" Why ?"

" I have been asked to call those at Aluth Walauwa that way "

" Anyway don't call me Appo ; if you call me Sunil, that's enough "

Galbanda's angry voice was heard again.

" Oh God, won't you all come today ?"

" They have already started coming there " shouted Ranmenika.

" Are your legs broken ?" asked Galbanda again.

" You go, I'll come later ", whispered Sunil into Nimal's ear. Sunil hid himself in the Kanda shrubbery and Nimal went to the stone quarry.

" Where is sister ?"

" She is said to have gone to pound paddy "

" Can you break stones alone until I tie the buffalo and come ?"

" I can "

" Then I'll come soon " said Galbanda and went away.

Nimal started crushing stones with a small hammer; when Galbanda's call to the buffaloes was heard in the distance Sunil slowly went towards Nimal.

" Give me also a hammer Nimal "

" You can't do these things, blisters will come on your palms"

" Then why do you break ?"

" I am used to this "

" I too will get used "

" What for ?"

" Then why do you break stones ?"

" To buy rice for us "

Sunil laughed.

" Why rice ?"

" To eat "

Sunil laughed more. He thought Nimal's answer was childish.

" Is rice bought by breaking stones ?"

" Rice is taken from paddy, paddy is taken from paddy fields"

" That is not the way Nimal. Stones are broken to be paved on the roads."

" Yes when stones are broken we get money ; from the money we buy rice. "

Sunil could not understand the argument. He too asked for a hammer and started breaking stones. But Sunil soon realized that he could not do the work carefully, nimbly and with ability. Before long Sunil's hand started paining.

" My hand is paining a great deal , Nimal "

" That is what I told you " said Nimal and laughed.

" Let me see your hand ?"

Nimal showed both his hands. Sunil who saw the corns that had come up on Nimal's palm was surprised. He compared Nimal's hand with his.

" Your hand is very soft " said Nimal stroking the palm.

Suddenly the noise of a car was heard. Sunil identified it by its sound.

" Its our car ; I'll hide "

Sunil went behind the heap of granite stones and hid himself. The Morris Minor car climbed the hill with a big noise. In it was Nelum Bandara and Maithri.

" I'll go Nimal , we'll meet tomorrow " he said and jumped on to the road and ran.

Chapter Five

The Kumarihami, Maha Kumarihami, the cook woman, Palingumenike, Maithri's maid Cecelia and the watcher Mudalihami looked for Sunil everywhere.

" Has he gone even towards the well, Mudalihami ?"

" What are you saying ! He hasn't gone there Dingirihamuduruwo."

" Go and look for him Palingumenika. Go to the top of the land and look. Putha! Putha! "

All looked for Sunil everywhere. For almost half an hour they looked for Sunil in the neighborhood.

" Don't cry Dingirihamuduruwo. Sudu Appo will be somewhere " said Mudalihami attempting to comfort her.

" He's not a baby. He's a boy of ten, isn't he ? He may have gone for a walk "

Although the Maha Kumarihami said this she quietly went inside the house and made a vow by making an offering.

" Where, even their Appachchi hasn't come yet " said Nelum Kumarihami and wiping her tears with the edge of the osariya she went down the steps and advanced towards the garage as the car arrived.

" Didn't you see our son? " the Kumarihami asked Nelum Bandara.

Nelum Bandara was a well built man of about forty years. His features resembled the Maha Kumarihami. His eyes were large and his forehead was broad. The hair was parted on the left and the hair on the crown of his head was thin. He wore a white shirt and a pair of brown trousers.

" Why? Didn't he come after school was closed ? " he asked without getting down from the car.

" He came; he even ate rice. After that we do not know where he went. Isn't it good to go even towards the town and look for him? " asked the Kumarihami.

" That's good " confirmed the grandmother.

" There Sunil malli is coming! " shouted Maithri looking through the rear glass of the car.

All looked in that direction. Sunil came running along the road.

" Don't say or do anything. We'll go home " said Bandara.

They all agreed.

" Let him come will you " said Kumarihami looking back and biting her teeth.

Nelum Bandara put his car in the garage, closed the door, and climbed the steps. Sunil too came quickly. They all sat in the veranda, pretending to be engaged in some other talk.

" It will take about a month or so to rain " said aththamma and took the betel box into her hands.

" When it rains it rains and when it is dry it remains dry" said the mother.

" There is no damage to the paddy fields although the sun shines now " said Mudalihami suppressing a smile.

" Palingumenika, bring a cup of tea here, will you " said appachchi.

Sunil too climbed on to the veranda but nobody took any

notice of him. They all continued to talk and talk about the rain. This made Sunil tired. He took a large quantity of guavas into his cupped hands and with a slight smile that made his face look pleasant looked around. No one took any notice of him. He coughed slightly; but none looked at him.

" Here appachchi guavas " said Sunil and walked towards him.

" Because we stay in the country we don't take any notice; how hot it would be in cities. " saying this and as if repeating something by heart appachchi took a guava into his hand. Still the elders did not stop the conversation.

" These are very tasty grandmother " said Sunil and held out both his hands.

" Throw that rubbish away "

" No grandmother, they are very sweet. "

She pushed aside Sunil who stood in front of her with her hand saying, " Towards Anuradhapura the earth may be scorched"

Sunil went towards the mother.

The mother too ignored him and took a guava, saying, "Towards Hambantota there may not be water even to drink "

Since no one asked him either about the guavas or the journey that he had made he could not bear it up any longer. He looked here and there with a face that looked as if he were about to cry.

The elderly people seeing him made signs among them and laughed secretly.

" Mother do you know from where these guavas are ? " Sunil, his face flushed, attempted to begin his story.

The mother, threw an empty look at him and then looked aside

" These , I plucked from Galwalewatte "

The mother was unable to hold back her anger any longer. She forgot the advice given by appachchi. She bristled with anger.

" Hereafter if you go anywhere without telling me, I'll tie you to a tree and beat you " she said as she stared at him.

Sunil was surprised, to get such a scolding. ' What wrong I have done?' he thought.

" Otherwise I shall hand you over to the police straight away, do you understand? " said the mother in a threatening voice.

Sunil who saw the fiendish look in her face said,

" Yes "

" Then go, wash your face and drink your tea "

" What, what is it ? " asked appachchi as if he did not know anything .

" How much did we go in search of him! Thinking that this fellow is lost "

" We were half dead after it " said the mother with a flushed face.

" Of course of course " started the grandmother

" Did a gypsy take him away? There are snakes here. The well is there. The stream is there. Who knows what happened "

" Come here " called appachchi.

Wiping both his eyes with both hands full of guavas Sunil went sobbing towards his father. When he went close to him, he burst out crying very loudly.

" Where did you go? "

" I went down the garden " answered Sunil crying.

The elders suppressed their laughter.

" Then I saw guavas and plucked them "

" Then why did you come along the road? "

" I climbed on to the road from a place close to the quarry"

" Haven't you done a big round! " said the mother in anger and fear and pride at the son's courage suppressing the faint smile that arose.

" Hereafter whenever you go you must tell me, do you hear?" demanded the father. By way of a reply he cried out louder. It was after his father asked him twice that he gave the promise.

" Go and wash your face " said the father.

Sunil went inside the house sobbing.

The elders laughed.

" What laughter, I'm telling you! Still my hands and legs have no life" said the mother.

" Never has he gone out like this before. That is why we got frightened " said the grandmother too.

Sunil went inside and after putting all the guavas on the table where plates were kept he threw himself on the bed.

That night he recounted his adventures to his sister Maithri before he slept.

Chapter Six

Nimal's house is called Galwalegedara. It is not a house but a hut. It was put up by Nimal's father, Muthu Banda. The ancestral home of the Galwalegedara people is Muthumale Walauwa. Muthumalegedera became Muhtumale Walauwa after Nimal's grandfather acquired the title of Basnayake Nilame.

Muthumale Basnayake Nilame was involved in a false murder case and in order to save himself he sold Muthumale Walauwa to a chettiyar and paid the proctor's fees. At the end of course he was acquitted in the case.

" It would have been very much better if I were sent to the gallows and saved this house. Then my boy who hasn't anybody to help him at least has the house to live in " said Basnayake Nilame. It was to Muthu Banda, his only son that he referred to as "My boy"

" Don't say that Nilame. If the thing that you call life goes out it's gone for good. The land is mere nothing " said the chettiyar feeling his stomach with the left hand and twisting his knot of hair with his right hand.

" However long we stay, what we call life somehow goes. Land is not that it must remain for those who come after us, "

" But in this, for Loku Nilame or Bandara Mahattaya or Bandara Mahattaya's son there will be no blame whatsoever from me even if they stay for any length of time. My tongue is only one not two "

But two months after the death of the Basnayake Nilame the chettiyar issued writ.

" Please chettiyar be patient till we give the almsgiving after the three months " pleaded Nimal's father Muthu Banda, now Galbanda.

" It is in the hands of the proctor; what can I do now! "

After that the chettiyar behaved as if deaf. Therefore Muthu Banda in two weeks time barely put up Galwalegedara and went to live in it with Ranmenika and the daughter Amitha. Nimal had not been born then.

The garden adjoining the quarry and the paddy field belonged to Muthu Banda then. But later these two were sold. That too because he got involved in a case.

The chettiyar who acquired the Muthumale Walauwa claimed ownership of the garden of the Walauwa too.

" Its only the Walauwa that appachchi sold. How could you become the owner of the garden? "

" You look at the deed Muthu Banda aiya. Am I to tell you lies and go to hell? "

" No you devil, only the Walauwa was written. "

" Bandara Mahattaya you still say it isn't "

" Ha! Then we'll go to court " said Muthu Banda and got out.

Muthu Banda went straight away and retained proctor Weerawickrama. If he takes a side he would not let down that side whatever happens. He had a reputation for that. His fees were high; his mouth sharp. Similarly victory is also certain

" If Weerawickrama is retained success is also certain", that was what people who have heard him say. Muthu Banda paid the proctor whatever he asked him from time to time without any hesitation.

Stamp fees, charges for copies of case proceedings, land registry search fees, proctor's fees, " those charges ", " these charges " and all other charges Muthu Banda paid without uttering a word. Towards the end he was showed doubt.

" Here are all your letters, go and get hold of a two penny proctor; you want to win the case and you also want to get it argued in court well and also want to get it done for a song. That chettiyar I understand wanted to retain me. If I took that man's side I wouldn't have any of these troubles " said Proctor Weerawickrama in one breath frothing from either side of his mouth.

" No, No sir, I am ready for whatever sum and whatever you say " said Muthu Banda putting his two palms together as if in worship.

" What else is there then! " said Proctor Weerawickrama trying to suppress his happiness. He then laughed loudly.

Muthu Banda found it difficult to obtain the money for the case. There was only one thing to be done and that was to mortgage some land. The only property he had was the paddy field and the garden close to the quarry. On one side Muthumale garden adjoined this property; and on the other side was the garden of Aluth Walauwa people. Therefore Muthu Banda thought that the people of Aluth Walauwa would gladly buy it On the other hand Muthu Banda thought of selling the property to a complete outsider If it was given to an outsider without giving to anyone in the village he would at least not lose his pride.

Coco Nana also had money. Moratu Mudalali near the bridge was looking for a land to build a house they said. But if this property which adjoins that of Nelum Bandara who works in the court is given to an outsider, his land case, he thought, would be adversely affected. On the other hand to whomsoever it is given it would be by way of a mortgage. When the costs of the land case are recovered the property could be completely bought back, he thought.

Muthu Banda conveyed his intention to Nelum Bandara and he in turn conveyed it to the Maha Kumarihami.

" There son, a good time has come " said the Maha Kumarihami very pleased when she heard the news" That fellow's father was the Basnayake. That fellow without giving the Muthumale Walauwa to us gave it to the chettiyar. Why? Because your father's brother, they say, sought a wife from them. Even at that time they opposed it on grounds of caste and said that it could not be done. They are a very jealous crowd. Now can't you see how they are losing even a place to dwell "

" Then are we buying the property or not? " asked the son.

" We must somehow buy it. We shall buy it by giving the money in driblets. Why should we get that property surrounded by our properties on a mortgage ".

" Don't say that mother! Now the new rich are looking out to grab properties here "

Somehow the Aluth Walauwa people got the paddy field and the garden close to the quarry on a mortgage.

Muthu Banda lost his land case. They all said that Proctor

Weerawickrama took the other side. Otherwise never does he lose a case.

" There is no reason to lose such a good case" said an old Proctor's clerk.

" This was because of the possibility of some harm coming to the proctor who wrote the fraudulent deed "

" Don't you know that Proctors don't go against other Proctors " said the person who pledged security for costs.

Muthu Banda later came to hear the truth, for when Proctor Weerawickrama built his house that chettiyar supplied bricks and cement free. It was common knowledge that this was in return for the help to the chettiyar.

Whether it was true or not Muthu Banda lost the land case. The judge gave the judgment with costs. Therefore the people of Muthumale Walauwa lost every thing. Nelum Bandara too stealthily helped the chettiyar. It was not solely because of his betel offerings but also because of the fact that if the chettiyar won the case it would not be possible for Muthu Banda to redeem the mortgage and the property would therefore finally devolve on Nelum Bandara.

Now Muthu Banda stays at Galwalewatta because of Nelum Bandara's generosity. He works the paddy field on "Ande" and breaks stones for wages. In the meantime after the birth of the eldest daughter Nimal and two daughters and two sons were born at Galwalegedara.

Chapter Seven

Earlier on the site of the present Aluth Walauwa there was Nelumwattegedara. After Maha Nelum Bandara was appointed Maha Korale the house came to be known as Korale Walauwa. Later after he made some money the old house was pulled down and a new house of modern design was built and they called it Aluth Walauwa.

" Now they talk about Walauwas! Formerly they tapped our trees " the Muthumale people insulted the Korale people. It was for this reason that they were unwilling even to give a daughter in marriage to them. " They talk boastfully after eating from the Devala. Formerly they were the people who looked after our elephants " The Korale Nilame conveyed this to them.

" What both parties say is correct. Both parties are equally big and equally small " said the high priest of the temple

" It is true that they tapped the trees of these people. That was how each generation became rich or poor " said the priest again to several devotees while crushing the betel chew in a little brass mortar.

From the time that the fortunes of the Muthumale Basnayake started declining the Korale of Nilamewatta began improving. Money and other things that the Basnayake Nilame received from the Devala were considerable. But nothing remained with him. He was involved in many law suits and disputes and it is said that in order to acquire the office of Basnayake he had to borrow a large sum of money.

Within a week of the death of the Basnayake, the Korale too died. It could be said that both died as a reason of old age. However the Basnayake was not so old as the Korale. But he appeared to be older. The reason for this was excessive drinking and getting involved in a murder case. Many said that the Basnayake got involved in the murder case because of the Korale. The Kapuralas and the Arachilas said that they died during the same week in order to be born in the same world of evil spirits.

" They say this through jealousy. In doing public service subordinates blaming the superiors is not a new thing. " people said.

" Son chase them out of that hut " said the Maha Kumarihami very often. But the son and the daughter did not listen to her.

" What won't people tell us? ". And since they fear people blaming them, both husband and wife remained silent

Nelum Bandara and Kumarihami have one daughter and one son. The daughter Maithri is in her eleventh year. She is big built and chubby. She takes after the father. Her eyes are big and the face is round. She has thin lips and a proud look. She is in the 6th standard at the Viharamaha Devi Vidyalaya.

" He is the only stripling who is there to buy me a cloth ". says the grandmother fondling Sunil whenever she gets into a mood

" What will you do son when you grow up? "

" I will be a policeman or a lory driver grandmother " says Sunil

The elders who hear this laugh But Sunil ignores it

Chapter Eight

Saturday dawned. Sunil was unable to forget Nimal. He began thinking of Nimal as he lay on the bed. Nimal had eaten roti on the previous afternoon. But Sunil had eaten rice. At school when eleven o'clock strikes Sunil gets two slices of buttered bread and a glass of milk. But Nimal stays without food. Sometimes he buys gram for a cent. Often he gives half of it to Sunil. On Friday evening if Sunil had allowed Nimal to eat the mango that fell on the swarm of blue flies Nimal's hunger would have been appeased.

Is it because Sunil was greedy that he fought for it? Or is it because he was naughty? If it were for any one of them it is wrong. After this Sunil would never do anything wrong again.

Sunil looked at the palm of his right hand. There were several blisters that had appeared on it. They were not large. They may not turn out to be wounds. Yet when fingers are bent they pained a little. How much would Nimal's hand pain?. Now it seems they did not pain. He had got used to it.

What a good pastime is breaking stones. After the large rocks are split by Galbanda Nimal with a small hammer breaks them into small pieces. It's not a very difficult thing to do. It's a fine pastime. It's true that the arm pains. What does it matter if it does not pain when you get used to it.

Breaking stones is not only a pastime but it is also a means of earning money, they say. How is that?

" Mother "

" Why? "

" Why do these people breaks stones? "

" Because they have sinned in their past births"

" It's not that. It's because they get money "

" Of course they get money "

" You get money not because you have sinned but because you have done merit "

" You break stones because you have sinned previously"

" Mother. may I too break stones? "

" Where? "

" In the quarry "

" Why? "

" I like it very much "

" You have not sinned "

" I have done sin "

" How do you know? "

" Because I get the desire to break stones "

" Go, Go, wash your face and drink your tea. You have come here to interpret "

Sunil started thinking again. Why doesn't his mother like him breaking stones?

Sunil washed his face, changed his clothes. drank his tea and stepped on to the courtyard.

" Brother. shall we play at ' Ambaata '? suggested Maithri.

" Please akka. I can't; my leg aches " said Sunil and sat down on the steps.

Maithri played at ' Ambaata '.

Sunil thought for a little while and went inside the house.

" Mother shall I go to pick guavas? "

" With whom? "

" Alone "

" Where? "

" Down the garden "

" Don't go far like yesterday. Now be careful. You must also come quickly "

" Please mother, may I too go ", begged Maithri

" Yes, carefully! "

Sunil was not pleased at this; yet he was silent. What Sunil wanted was not to eat guavas but to meet Nimal. Sunil did not want to go and meet Nimal with Maithri. Maithri laughs at beggars. She mimics Tikiri who collects firewood. She jokes with Letchchimi who plucks tea. She beats and scolds Cecilia without any reason. She pinches her, She eats lozenges without giving her while she looks on. Therefore if Maithri sees Nimal's hut she will laugh and put Nimal to shame. She is a tale carrier. Whatever happens she will tell mother everything that happens. Mother will praise her for this. And if Maithri describes some incident it will always be unfavourable to others.

" We must not call her Maithri but Napuri " the mother tells her when she sees her cruelty.

Maithri is a beautiful girl. At a glance all will think that the name will suit her. But when one associates with her for some time her name proves to be the opposite. She tortures the butterflies. She also tries to kill flies. Mother scolds her saying. "These may be what is taught to you at school ".

Therefore Sunil did not go very far with Maithri akka. He went up to the fence, plucked two guava fruits from a tall tree and turned back.

Chapter Nine

On Monday morning Sunil and Maithri got into their appachchi's car and went to school. After going a little distance Sunil saw Nimal. Nimal clad in a khaki shirt, a blue pair of shorts and wearing a brown pair of canvas shoes was hastily going along with two bundles of books tightly pressed against his two sides.

" Appachchi we'll put that boy too and go "

Appachchi stopped the car.

" Nimal " called Sunil.

Nimal stood on the edge of the road and looked as if he had turned to stone.

" Get in " said appachchi not because he recognized him but because of Sunil's request. Nimal got in to the rear seat. Since he got into the car as if he got into a cart by placing both his feet his head stuck the door. Maithri saw this and laughed out loud. Sunil in anger pinched her secretly. Nimal stroking his head wiped the perspiration that came down his forehead with the shirt sleeve.

" Boy, are you also in my son's class? " asked appachchi.

" Yes ", said Sunil.

After this there wasn't any conversation, Sunil was frightened thinking that appachchi would ask him about his parents. But he did not ask him anything.

Maithri with a disgusting look which made her beautiful face look ugly pushed herself to the corner of the seat and sat down. She observed coconut oil trickling down close to Nimal's ears and she laughed. Sunil stared hard at her.

Sunil thought of sharing the two slices of bread and the glass of milk that he received that day with Nimal. Nimal did not agree. He said that Sudu Appo's food is for Sudu Appo.

" Don't call me Sudu Appo. If the boys hear it they will jeer at us "

" If appachchi hears it I'll get a beating "

" Appachchi is not here "

Sunil tried very hard to give a slice of bread to Nimal. At last Nimal accepted it.

But afterwards Nimal for several days hid himself in the lavatory and went into the class-room by going along the playground, getting on to the main road and returning back to the class-room.

" Then I too will not eat " he threatened and Nimal had to share the bread with him. Once they got used to it Nimal did not feel anything wrong. Nimal received it and also ate it without being seen by any one. It also remained between these two as a lasting secret.

That day when school closed the two friends as was their habit went together. It may be that because all had forgotten the incident that took place on Friday no one spoke about it. But on the surface of Sunil's mind what remained still was the incident of the shameful fight.

When they almost reached the mango tree Sunil spoke to his friends. " Now hereafter, we will not fight for mangoes. We will not compete in races. We will not compete in picking mangoes. Whoever picks them will collect them together and will divide them and eat ". All accepted the proposal.

" Of course yes; this thought occurred to me too. Even crows eat after dividing the food among them without quarrelling "

" We are worse than crows " said one boy.

The proposal was put in to effect. The unity of the group of boys was strengthened some more.

As Sunil and Nimal approached the stone quarry Galbanda kept the sledge hammer on the ground as on the previous day. He curved the right forefinger and wiped away the perspiration from his scarred forehead.

" That's how you must be. If you do any harm to Sudu Appo you may tell me so "

Sunil got angry. Of what use is the help of others?. Why don't the elders know that the differences that friends have could be settled among themselves. Yet a thought flashed in his mind.

" Nimal does one wrong "

" What is it? " asked Galbanda and looked at the Hinguru bush.

Nimal too widened his eyes and looked at Sunil.

" You call me ' Sudu Appo ' "

A lump of saliva went down Nimal's throat. The suffocating breath again flowed with ease.

Galbanda too laughed.

" Sudu Appo, I am the one who had asked him to call you that way"

" Ask him not to call me that "

" That's not good. Respectable people must be honoured. that is a custom of the Sinhala people "

" I don't know. Don't call me that. The boys will laugh at us"

" Son, then call Sudu Appo by what he wants "

" Yes "

" Call mother and the others to break stones. Today you better study "

Nimal went down the slope and went away. Sunil too went towards his house.

How much frightened is Nimal of Galbanda?. Even for a little fault of Nimal Galbanda first looks at the Hinguru bush. How frightened was he when he was there!. He was greatly agitated. He was frightened as if he had seen a ghost.

Sunil's parents always addressed him kindly. Even when he does some wrong often he is made to sit on the lap and is admonished.

He does not remember when he had been beaten even once. Sometimes his mother takes two ' Ekels ' and reproaches him. But he has never been beaten.

Sunil sat at the dining table.

" Am I to feed you son? " asked his mother coming towards him, tying her knot of hair: She had a newspaper in her hand.

" No mother, I'll eat "

" My son is big now. That's how he should be " she said and kissed his head.

" The perspiration in your head! Can't you wait in school son until appachchi's car comes?

" I can't. I can come walking. Mother shall I go walking in the morning also? "

" How tired you will be. Keep quiet without trying to be deceptive "

The first mouthful he put into his mouth choked him. His mother made him drink some water. When food chokes mother, she says "Appachchi may be hungry still "

" Nimal may not have rice today too ". Yet he didn't say anything.

Mother read the newspaper. Sunil ate the food thoughtfully. He is quite hungry. But he was unable to fill his stomach fully.

" Why son, have you finished eating? " asked the mother seeing the son washing his hand.

" Yes "

" Cecelia bring the papaws "

Cecelia then brought half of a fully ripe papaw. Sunil without enjoying its taste swallowed it.

" Ah Punchi Mama came today " she said and opened the safe and took out two small pieces of cake decorated with sugar and chocolate, and kept on a dish saying

" These are what he brought "

" Are both these pieces for me? "

" Yes, we ate, there is still more "

" I will eat a little later "

" You may eat whenever you like my son "

Chapter Ten

Sunil rose from the table and going towards the barn, fondled
Neela, the dog.He swung his tail to and fro like pilgrims who
go to temple on dark poya days through the paddy fields to
listen to bana preaching swinging lighted fronds.

" Neela did you eat rice? Ah, did you eat rice? " asked
Sunil.

The dog as if trying to talk uttered " ow ".

Yes Neela must have eaten rice. Rice has been left in its enamel
plate. But Nimal? Sin!. Sunil was again occupied in thought.

" Mother, shall I go to pluck some guavas " asked Sunil
after going into the house.

" What guavas son every day? Sleep a little will you to
get rid of your tiredness "

" Only today mother; I'll come back quickly "

" Then come soon. Like the other day we can't be looking for you, mind you "

Sunil went quietly and put the two pieces of cake inside a
paper bag and stepped on to the courtyard. As if a thought had
dawned on him he went back into the house and took the reed
flute which was on a shelf in his room. It was the flute that he
bought last term for the musical show at school. He hid both
the flute and the parcel and stepped into the open.

His grandmother was asleep as usual. Cecilia and
Palingumenika were seated in the kitchen and were playing

'Olinda ' on the sly. Sunil went down the garden up to the fence and climbed the guava tree. He kept his foot on one branch and sat on a forked branch.

It was not only the shanty on the slope but also a part of the quarry that could be seen well from there. The sound of the sledge- hammer too could be heard. The silvery water of the stream that falls down the stone ledge and flows down too could be clearly seen.

Sunil took the reed flute and blew the tune that Radha and Krishna had played in the school drama. He heard the echo. In a moment Nimal came out to the courtyard and looked up. Sunil smiled a little and continued to blow the flute. Nimal rushed into the house. He too brought his flute and played the tune which was the reply. What arose from this was an invitation from Nimal asking Sunil to come down. Little by little Sunil went down the slope. He was able to go a little faster than on the previous day. After he had gone some distance Sunil called out loudly to him.

" Nimal come here "

" There is no one at home; I have got to look after my brothers and sisters " answered Nimal.

Sunil went down to the extreme end. He saw four children playing about in the courtyard. Two out of them had no cloths on their bodies. Out of the other two one wore a dirty torn shirt and the other a similar gown. The children seeing Sunil took coconut shells and Akkapana leaves and went towards a corner of the courtyard and began playing at ' cooking rice. '

" Here, Nimal " said Sunil and held out the paper bag.

" What is it? " asked Nimal, and without taking it he looked on. Sunil then went forward and kept it in his hand.

Nimal opened it and after examining it said, " Please don't bring these " and held out the bag to Sunil. The three year old naked girl who saw this came running towards him.

" Brother, give me also theen ball " she said and stretched out her hand.

" Come here Leela " said the four year old girl. She caught her hand and pulled her.

" For me, for me " said the other naked one who also came running.

" Here, here " said the five year old boy wearing a shirt and catching him by the shoulder.

" Go away, go away, go and play " said Nimal and pushed all four away.

" Nimal leave them alone will you " said Sunil and going close to them asked " Leela, did you eat rice? "

" No rice, ate thothee "

Sunil thought that he was choked with food earlier as a reason of that.

" Will it rain today? " asked Nimal attempting to change the conversation in some other direction.

" Looks it " said Sunil and put his hand into the paper bag and broke the two pieces of cake into five and distributed them among the four children.

" What's this? " asked Neela.

" It's bread, bread " said Nimal.

Sunil gave the remaining piece with the bag to Nimal. Nimal was looking on absorbed in thought. Sunil was thinking whether Nimal would kick his hand just like how Sunil kicked the mango.

Nimal heaved a sigh and took the bag.

" I shall keep this for my sister " he said

" This is not bread brother, they are buns " said small Leela stammering.

Sunil who watched the little children for a little while said " Mother and others will look for me. I'll go "

He then went up the garden.

Chapter Eleven

When Sunil stepped into the house his father had already arrived. Just as on other days he took his tea in the veranda. On a dish was a piece of cake.

" Do you want it son? "

" I ate appachchi "

" If you want eat it "

" Don't you want it appachchi? "

" Don't try to be clever, if you want it please eat it "

" Then I will eat it later " he said and took the dish into the house. He then put the piece of cake into another paper bag and placed the paper bag in the school bag and came outside.

" Mother tell brother not to take odd fellows in our car" said Maithri akka grumbling.

" Whom did you take son? "

" A boy from our class "

" She says odd fellows! "

" But what about odd girls she takes "

" Do we take those dripping with coconut oil and smelling of body odour. That fellow did not even know how to get into the car. I thought he cracked his skull when he got into the car ", said Maithri and smiled in anger.

Sunil stared at her.

" Who is that boy son? "

" He is the one who is first in our class "

" If he is the first the others would be like snake charmers "

" That is in your hopper boutique school "

" Our school is not like your parippu school ".

Since it is a sin to beat her Sunil bore it up.

" Cruel Maithri, cruel Maithri Hu, hu "

" Sunil sudda, Sunil sudda. Enough for you, enough for you " said Maithri by way of tit for tat.

" Goda suddhi, cruel Maithri, goda suddhi, cruel Maithri", repeated Sunil like a broken gramophone record and sat on mother's lap.

Maithri became docile and leaned against appachchi saying "Just see appachchi "

" Go away both of you; If I take a stick I'll beat both of you" threatened appachchi.

Both become silent. Maithri looked at Sunil from the corner of her eyes. He made faces at her. He looked at her. She also made faces at him and left the place.

" Cruel Maithri, cruel Maithri " said Sunil in a low tone.

The mother heard it and pushed him away from her lap. He smiled coyly and climbed back to his mother's lap. Appachchi, mother, grandmother put on grave faces and engaged themselves in a discussion.

" What are you thinking so much; if you are transferred you have to go " said the mother in a tone of finality.

" Although you say so how troublesome it is to stay in Kandy. Everything is for money isn't it. Can you break a stick for firewood? Can you pluck a handful of pala? Can you give a cup of tea to a person and get a log of wood split for firewood?

Can you get a coconut tree plucked? Everything is for money "
said grandmother.

" You cannot travel from here, can you? " asked the
mother from appachchi.

" Forty miles up and down; I'll get killed after driving
the car " said appachchi as if he had lost all hope.

" Take a driver " said Sunil, as a suggestion to solve
the question of driving the car not knowing the seriousness of
the discussion.

" A salary to the fellow! Petrol for the car! My labour"
said appachchi.

This gave Sunil some courage since he realized that the idea
he expressed was not one without any sense.

" Shall we tell the M.P. even and see " asked the grandmother.

" That man will say ' Yes ' for anything. But nothing
will happen. " said appachchi as if in anger.

" What is it mother? " Sunil asked in a low tone.

" Appachchi is transferred to Kandy. "

" So? "

" We may all have to go after taking a house in Kandy. "

" What a good thing it is "

The three elders who heard it looked at one another and smiled.
Sunil who was encouraged by this said, " Please appachchi it's
good there "

" What difficulties have they? " said appachchi and
laughed more.

" Mother, from when are we going there? "

" Not next month; but on the first of the month after
next. "

" It's really good. There we will be able to see the Perahera. We can also go round the lake ", said Sunil showing a happy face.

But his happiness vanished in a moment. That was because he remembered Nimal. When Nimal is not there what happiness is there for him, he thought.

" In a way we don't want Kandy, mother. It's better here " said Sunil embracing the mother's neck.

" Now this time why is that? " asked the mother.

" Nothing, this is our home, isn't it, after all. "

Chapter Twelve

The friendship that Sunil had towards Nimal gradually improved. Sunil had pity on Nimal. He was also kind to him. He wished Nimal success, happiness, comfort and good health.

There is no doubt that those who knew of their friendship thought that it is a wonderful attachment. But no one knew of its depth. Muthu Banda of the stone quarry and Ranmenika knew that Sudu Appo and Nimal were friends. When school closes they knew that they would come home together. It is also known that Sunil treats Nimal as if he is one like him.

There is also much that they do not know. If Sunil gets something new to eat half of it would be put inside the school bag and given to Nimal the following day; if it could not be kept till the following day, with the help of the reed flute he gets him up to the guava tree or if there are no elders in the house he goes there and gives it to him.

If Sunil gets money from his appachchi, mother or grandmother to eat gram, lozenges, Gal siyambala or Nelli he shares it with Nimal.

At the beginning Nimal did not like it. " Sunil can I take these things this way every day like a beggar? " asked Nimal one day.

" When I have I give you. When I don't have and when you have you give me " said Sunil like a mature person.

" But I never have isn't it? "

" Why you give me Mora. You give me Lovi, Jambu ... "

" What are those? "

" How many days will there be in the future? Grandmother says there will still be an Asankeiya "

" They say no. The young priest says there will still be
Asankeiyas of Asankeiyas " said Nimal.

" That is it; so how many days have you got? " Sunil
argued.

As time passed Nimal accepted the small gifts that Sunil gave.
But Sunil was frightened to tell anything about Nimal at home.
When he remembered how mother laughed mentioning
Galbanda, how grandmother closed her ears after hearing that
Galbanda's son is in his class, how Maithri laughed that day
when Nimal came in the car, he did not have the courage to tell
anything about Nimal.

The annual prize giving of Gemunu Vidyalaya also drew
closer. This time too, the class prize was to be given to Nimal.
It was also revealed that Sunil too was getting a prize.

Two weeks before the prize giving the class teacher addressed
the class.

" Our prize giving this time is very close now; the last
Friday of this month; only two more weeks. All the children
must come dressed well in clean clothes. You all know what the
dress is; White shirt, Blue shorts, Black shoes and the school
tie. Did you understand? Specially Nimal and Sunil must come
dressed well. Why? Because these two are getting prizes. The
rest also must come dressed well. You must keep the honour of
our class and also that of the school. Did you all understand?"

" Yes " said all the children.

" Did you understand Nimal? "

" Yes "

" Sunil "

" Yes "

Immediately after Sunil went home he broke the good news to his mother that he was going to get a prize. The mother embraced him and carried him towards the grandmother's room.

" Set me on the ground, set me on the ground " he cried throwing his arms and legs about. This was because grandmother would scold him saying, " Trying to be a baby "

" Then we will have to cook Kavum and rub his arms and legs " said grandmother.

Appachchi who heard the news was very much pleased and he ordered six new suits to be made. Ten days passed. One day Sunil and Nimal were coming alone towards the quarry when Nimal stopped suddenly.

" Sunil "

" Ah " he said and put on a frightened look.

" Nothing, I merely wanted to know what would happen if I don't go to school on the day prizes are given? "

" Shame, that's not good "

" If I am unable to come that day, for instance, by falling sick? "

" What can be done for that? "

" Then what happens to the prize? "

" It will be given to you on another day. "

" I will not lose the prize, will I? "

" No "

The two friends resumed their journey again.

" Are your clothes and things ready? " asked Sunil

" Not yet "

" Did you tell your father, Nimal? "

" I told him "

" So? "

" He said he'll look into it "

What Nimal said was a lie. Sunil did not know that. But Sunil's subtle mind became aware that Nimal will not have the clothes that are needed .

When Sunil went home that day he saw his mother sitting on the lower step close to the threshing floor looking at the paddy being threshed. On seeing Sunil she stood up from the parapet wall connecting the steps and climbing the steps she went away holding Sunil's hand.

" There son your clothes have been brought today "

Sunil was silent.

" Why don't you talk? Are you angry because the clothes have been brought? "

" No "

" Then? "

" Mother why do I get so many clothes? "

" You have gifted clothes in your previous birth; that's the reason "

" To whom "

" To priests and those who had no clothes "

" Don't be silly, just keep quiet. Let me see, I want you to wear one ".

Sunil wore it while engaged in thought. The suit had been stitched well.

" Please mother, out of this six I shall give one to a boy"

" Who is this boy? "

" Mother does not know him. He hasn't got clothes. May be sometimes he may not come to the prize giving. "

" Ask appachchi and if he likes, give him "

" Please mother, I can't; you ask him and tell me mother"

" Eat your rice will you "

As he ate the food he urged his mother again and again about his request.

" Yes, yes, yes ", said the mother, maybe to avoid him fretting.

" Then I'll give one "

" Haven't I said yes? "

" If father scolds me? "

" Haven't I told you that I'll look after that "

" Good mother, good mother " said Sunil. He climbed the chair and keeping the food stained right hand out of reach embraced his mother's neck with his left hand and kissed her face.

" There, you have smeared my face with food " she said in pretence and wiped her face with the edge of her sari.

Chapter Thirteen

The sheaves of paddy that were being threshed in the lower threshing floor were from the paddy field near the stone quarry. That field which was being worked by Muthu Banda on Ande belong to Aluth Walauwa. That day being a Friday Sunil went down the steps without changing his clothes.

" Mother, I am going down to the threshing floor "

" Carefully. " Before the mother could give him permission he had gone down several steps. Sunil did not immediately recognize. Galbanda who was wearing a banian, a sarong and had tied a large handkerchief around his head. He was making a broom with twigs.

" Did our boy too come? " he asked respectfully.

" He came "

" Then why didn't he still come down to drive the buffaloes? For this kind of work he is very lazy. To him it is always the lessons "

Then Nimal would be coming to the threshing floor. How good it is. When they threshed paddy they go on till daybreak. Yesterday was Pasaloswaka Poya day. Therefore the moon will rise from over the hills. Good day. No rain too. Because it is Saturday there will be no school the following day. Sunil was swinging his legs and seated filled with keen anxiety.

" Is it true Sudu Appo that our boy is the first this time too?"

" Yes '

" I don't know whether he copies " said Muthu Banda.

Another farmer who heard this smiled and said, " Then it may be so"

" He is a person who does not copy " said Sunil angrily and firmly.

" Sudu Appo loves our boy very much but it appears as if our boy does not take any notice of him " said Muthu Banda taking the hay fork in his hand.

" No, he also loves me " said Sunil and stood opposing him.

" Then it doesn't matter. When he gets angry he is good for nothing "

" All say that he is good " said Sunil.

The two farmers who heard this stopped their work, pinned their hay forks on the ground, looked at each other's face and smiled.

" Can't you see, he does not speak one word against him " said Muthu Banda to his friendly farmer in a low voice.

" That is true " said the farmer shaking his head " some are used to it from a tender age "

The seven buffaloes tied to the heap of sheaves of paddy stalks went round and round eating stalks of paddy. The ' muduna ' had to go in a small circle. The buffalo tied there was elderly as well as experienced. It was that buffalo which bore the weight of all the others and was also responsible for the conduct of the others. It was the leader of all the buffaloes. The one which was tied last was a sturdy young buffalo. He had to run more than any one of them. It was he who received most of the beatings. A boy of the size of Sunil drove the buffaloes.

" Sudu Appo can't you drive the buffaloes? " asked Muthu Banda.

" What is it? "

" To drive the buffalos like this? "

" If they butt me? "

" You are driving them from behind " said the other farmer.

" They won't butt but it is the other job that Sudu Appo cannot do"

" What's that? "

" It's that " said Muthu Banda and stretched his arm. Sunil looked in the direction. He saw the boy that drove the buffaloes clearly take the cow dung dropped by a buffalo on to a pad of hay with his hands.

" Sudu Appo can you? " asked the boy smiling and taking the cow dung dropped by the buffalo on to a pad of hay, threw it into a lower paddy field.

" Of course I can't " said Sunil smiling. The others too smiled.

" There comes your friend " said Muthu Banda.

Nimal was coming in their direction. Sunil waved his hand at Nimal. Yet Nimal felt exceedingly shy and only smiled slightly. He was clad in a sarong, a banian and had tied a belt around his waist. He also had a handkerchief round his neck. Sunil who saw this thought if he too could dress like that. Nimal without coming towards Sunil went directly to the threshing floor.

The person who drove the buffaloes placed a bent forefinger in his ear, stiffened his nerves, opened his mouth and raising his voice sang, "Go on the peak my appo, uvo...uvo ". Sunil and Nimal hearing it looked at one another and smiled.

" Can't Sudu Appo sing to the buffaloes like that? " asked Galbanda.

Sunil smiled.

" Nimal, come come I'm tired " said the boy who drove the buffaloes. Sunil was surprised. Sunil seeing that Nimal could drive the buffaloes and he couldn't felt shy. Nimal was also very conversant with the language of the buffaloes. He also used words like "Ho, Ho, He Jah, Udi Baha " and many others too.

The moon was rising. The crows flew towards the garden crying. The frogs cried like young goats. Crickets surpassed few police whistles blown at once. In a distant paddy field a she buffalo was calling the young one that had strayed. Sunil who had been silently watching all that time asked Muthu Banda " Shall I also drive the buffaloes? "

" If you can what a good thing it is. Then both can drive together " said Muthu Banda and gave a new goad to Sunil. Sunil also took it and trampling the sheaves of paddy followed the buffaloes.

" Sunil you look after the three at the top. I will drive the others " said Nimal. The two shared the buffalos accordingly.

" You can't do that Sudu Appo. You must talk to the buffaloes. Otherwise they will fall asleep " said Muthu Banda.

" Udi, ho, Jaha " said Sudu Appo and smiled.

After a little while the father, mother, grandmother and Maithri came to see the threshing.

" Look at that " said the mother showing Sunil.

The other visitors started laughing.

" That is the way " said Muthu Banda laughing and others who saw him laughing also laughed very loud.

" Why does he want to cut the soles of his feet by moving about among the sheaves of paddy " grumbled the grandmother.

" Good that they get to learn these things " said the father.

" We have got many people for the harvest to day Menike " said Muthu Banda looking at the new-comers and smiling.

Sunil seeing his people and feeling shy and consequently discouraged came out of the threshing floor.

" Eiya Govirala, Eiya govirala " shouted Maithri as if singing a song.

" So what does it matter to you sister? "

" Govirala Gongahawwa, Govirala Gongahawwa " bantered Maithri again.

" Polkitchi Rawatichchi, Cruel Maithri " said Sunil

" See will you "

" Then, why does he call me? "

" Shut your mouths, both of you " rebuked the grandmother.

After a little while about seven or eight farmers with hay forks gathered at the threshing floor. While engaged in conversation about all sorts of things they separated the sheaves of the outer circle and put them on to the peak of the hay cock.

Nimal and the other boy drove the buffaloes round in turns and threshed the corn.

At the tea - factory on the top of the hill they heard eight ' o'clock being struck, Mudalihami carrying a cane basket descended the steps and came towards the threshing floor. Palingumenika came behind him carrying a pot on her hip and a brass sembuwa in her hand.

" Muthettuwa too has been brought " said grandmother.

" We'll also go. I am also very hungry "

" Since Sudu Appo took part in the threshing his share of Muthettuwa is there " said Muthu Banda.

Chapter Fourteen

The following morning Sunil washed his face, changed his clothes, ate his breakfast and came towards the threshing floor. The threshing floor was empty. The buffaloes were grazing on the paddy field ridges. The threshed paddy was collected in the centre into a cone. It was covered with straw. In the hut at the corner of the threshing floor someone was sleeping. Along the edge of the threshing floor the ridge of straw had been stacked.

Sunil walked around the cone of paddy. A good quantity of paddy had got stuck in the threshing floor. Sunil with the toe of his right foot loosened a few grains of paddy and brought them to the surface. He then heard a voice from the direction of the hut.

" It's daylight, get up, get up. " It was Muthu Banda.

Those who were sleeping close to him got up and sat on the mats. They cleaned their eyes and faces with both hands and made themselves tidy.

" What! it's Nimal isn't it? " Sunil went towards the hut.

" Ha, Sudu Appo! There, our work is now over " said Muthu Banda showing the heap of paddy looking like a cone.

" Son, I shall come after washing my face " he said and left the threshing floor.

" Nimal "

Nimal who wiped his face with the cloth with which he had tied his head smiled at Sunil.

" Didn't you go home last night? " asked Sunil.

" When the threshing was over four o'clock struck in the factory. "

" Until then you did not sleep? "

" I slept for short periods "

Sunil was amazed. How sleepy would he be!

" Nimal may be hungry too isn't it? "

" No, at two 'o'clock we ate ' imbul kiribath ' "

At the breakfast table too there was imbul kiribath for Sunil He thought that it was his share.

Nimal broke a stick from a Karanda tree close by, bit the end and made a brush of it and cleaned his teeth. He then stepped into the stream and walked in it here and there.

" Since I broke rest I feel feverish " said Nimal.

" In vain; how much I tried to come last night. My grandmother did not allow me to come "

" How good you didn't come, it was very cold here last night. Apart from that towards morning it rained. I too got partly wet. And I have got a cold " he said and sneezed.

A woman and a girl kept on coming towards the threshing floor.

" Who is that? " asked Sunil.

" Mother and sister "

" Yes it's true; Nimal's mother isn't it? I of course, haven't seen your sister. What's your sister's name? "

" Amitha "

" Beautiful name "

Amitha was about twelve years old. She wore a cloth and a jacket. Anybody could tell at a glance that she must be Nimal's sister.

" Son are you hungry? " asked Ranmenika and came into the hut with the daughter.

" Not much "

" When Appo is there it isn't lonely " said Ranmenika opening the parcel of rice. In an enamel plate, there was hunusal rice and a lunumiris sambol. Amitha too kept a pot of tea and a packet of sugar in the hut.

" Appachchi went home didn't he? " asked Nimal.

" Yes, appachchi will eat at home and come. If you keep some tea that's enough " said Ranmenika.

" Then I shall eat " said Nimal and looked at Sunil.

" Yes eat...eat; I ate ", said Sunil and kept on looking at his friend. Saliva spontaneously went down his throat. Thinking that Nimal's stomach would get spoilt he looked away.

Amitha having taken the tea pot poured tea into the enamel cup and kept it aside. She then took the little packet of sugar to her hand and uttered something into her mother's ear.

" Put it and give " Ranmenika too said in an undertone. Amitha took a little sugar on to her palm and putting it into the cup " Dissolve and drink " said Amitha and placed it close to Nimal. In the meantime Ranmenika and Amitha took two pieces of cloth and covered their heads. Then each took the upper ends and folded the cloth back and tied round their heads and left the other two ends to drop down. Then they tucked their cloths and went down to the threshing floor.

After they finished drinking tea Nimal got up and took his father's table knife from where it was hidden in the roof of the hut and removed it from the sheath. Then he stepped into the paddy field and cut off a stem of a paddy stalk and made a flute which he gave Sunil. Sunil then blew the flute.

" I want to see it? How did you make it? " asked Sunil. He too then learnt from Nimal how to make reed flutes and got two of them made for himself.

" There, there, appachchi is coming; I'll go to dry the hay " said Nimal and he went to the hut and stuck the knife in the roof.

" Nimal I too shall go and come " said Sunil and hastily went away climbing the steps.

Sunil had no mind to go home. He was not used to the work in the threshing floor. Yet like Nimal, by getting a small hay fork he did not think that he could turn the hay this side and that But it is possible that Ranmenika and Muthu Banda will laugh It's worse if grandmother sees it since she will not fail to chide him Therefore with bent head Sunil went home

Chapter Fifteen

At about four in the evening the paddy in the threshing floor was winnowed. Grandmother and mother came towards the threshing floor. Sunil too came with them.

" Don't come son, when dust gets into your nose you'll get a cough " said grandmother and attempted to prevent him from coming.

" Then why are other boys staying? "

" You are not like them "

" Why don't they get a cough? "

" They are used to it. This fellow is not only mature but also ripe. If something is said he'll ask a thousand questions " said grandmother without any patience.

Maithri listened to grandmother and remained at the Walauwa itself.

" My daughter is the only one who listens to me "

" That's because she is Suddhi " said Sunil.

" You go wherever you want; don't provoke her " said grandmother with affection and patted his back once. With that force Sunil went down a few steps and ran away.

" Slowly, slowly, I am frightened " said the mother.

In one corner of the threshing floor Ranmenika and Amitha were winnowing ' bol '.

Sunil watched with great interest the winnowing of the paddy

One person took the paddy in a winnowing pan and spread the paddy in the centre of the threshing floor in the shape of a rainbow. Then Muthu Banda and another person fanned the paddy with two winnowing pans walking backwards from one end to the other end. Then the third man took paddy in a winnowing pan just as before and spread the paddy on the same rainbow shaped stretch of paddy. The winnowers walked backwards fanning the paddy from one end to the other.

Ranmenika and Amitha collect the ' bol ' thrown out by the winnowing and winnow the ' bol ' to take out good grains of paddy mixed with ' bol '.

Nimal was looking at what his parents were doing.

The grandmother then called him.

" Come here patiya "

Nimal came. Sunil did not like the manner in which grandmother called him. Therefore his face turned red. As a reason of grandmother's arrogant talk Sunil feared that Nimal would sometimes be displeased with him.

" What is your name? " asked aththamma.

" Don't be rude. Speak kindly " said Sunil to aththamma in a low voice.

" Go away without coming to teach me " she said and stared at him.

" What's your name patiya ? " asked the grandmother.

" Nimal "

" Your name is too small, why didn't you tell your father to give you a bigger name? Do you go to school? "

" Yes "

" The school close to the village? "

" No "

" Then? "

" To Gemunu Vidyalaya "

" Ha, Ha, then you can't be without those names; isn't that so? You need trousers and shoes " said grandmother.

Nimal did not understand her ridicule. Sunil of course became aware that it was not said in good faith.

" Ah Muthu Banda " began grandmother again.

" Menike " said Muthu Banda who was taking some rest came there. The other two farmers also started listening.

" No, what I was telling your son; what's this that you are doing! What you are doing is just like a short cow running after the others that are running "

" Why Menike? "

" Without teaching them how to use the kathy and the Mammoty you are sending them to colleges "

" That's what I told him " confirmed a friendly farmer.

" The swelling must be according to the size of the finger " said the other farmer.

" It is by trying to do these things that you have suffered so much. You have not learnt still " said the grandmother as if in anger.

" No Menike; this fellow is always the first in the class they say. I wanted him to leave school several times; but the boy does not like it "

" You cannot do things according to what they say "

" That's of course true, Menike. Both the lady teachers and the teachers who teach him are also against his leaving "

" To what Kachcheri are you sending him to be a clerk"

" I don't know Menike "

" Those do not concern us. Is it going to hurt us? Do that work will you. " Grandmother stopped her talk. And Muthu Banda started winnowing the paddy with greater force than before.

Nimal too left the place slowly and stepped into the stream and washed his face which was flushed red.

There is no other unkind person than grandmother who interferes with the affairs of the others thought Sunil who even decided to scold her.

" Grandmother " said Sunil harshly and in anger, and softening the voice a little said " very bad " and climbed the steps and went home.

Chapter Sixteen

On Monday Nimal did not come for tea. Sunil went in search of him. Nimal was in the class-room itself.

" Come Nimal we'll have tea "

" From today don't call me for tea Sunil "

" Why? "

" I can't "

" What's the reason? "

Nimal remained thoughtful for a moment.

" Sunil why is your grandmother angry with me? "

" She is not angry with you "

" Then why did she tell my appachchi to remove me from school? "

" Our grandmother is mad "

" Is it true? "

" Yes, my mother also says sometimes that she is mad"

" Then am I to tell my appachchi that Sunil's grand-mother is mad "

" Tell him, tell him "

" I am of course aware of that. I felt very sad. Without doing any wrong to her why is she angry with me and trying to prevent me from going to school."

" Grandmother is mad. Come we will go and have tea "

Both went and as before they shared the bread and drank tea.

Sunil was unable to decide easily how to give Nimal the clothes that were set aside for him. If they are given as a present from Sunil Nimal may not accept them. Even if he accepts them Sunil's grandmother may come to know of it. If that happens Sunil will not fail to get scoldings and sarcastic remarks from her. Therefore Sunil wondered how he should do it.

Wednesday too came. The prize giving was on Friday; clothes for Nimal had not been stitched yet. Even if his father had money now of course there was no time to get the clothes stitched. Nimal's idea was not to go to school on Friday by pretending to be sick. Sunil thought that it would be better for Nimal not to come rather than be a target for the ridicule of the proud students by coming for the prize giving wearing dirty faded tight clothes.

An idea dawned on Sunil. Immediately he finished drinking the tea he went towards the teachers room. He went and stood near the door.

" Sunil, do you want to meet me? " asked the fifth class teacher.

" Yes "

She came out.

" They say that Nimal is not coming for the prize giving "

" Why "

" He hasn't got clothes "

" Why, will not his father get them stitched for him? "

" His father has no money " said Sunil looking at the floor sadly.

The class teacher was engaged in thought. Sunil resumed his

conversation.

" I asked my mother a new suit saying that I want to give it to a friend of mine. If I give it to Nimal he will not take it. "

" Why? "
" He does not like to take gifts from me "
" Did you try to give it? "
" No "
" Then "
" If teacher gives it he'll take "
" Saying it's a gift from me? "
" Yes "
" Good; when are you bringing it? "
" Tomorrow "
" Good "

Sunil went back with great pride.

The next day in the morning Sunil wrapped the suit carefully and took it to school. Without going into the class-room he went straight to the teachers room. The teacher was there expecting him.

" Did you bring it? "
" Yes "

Sunil gave the parcel to her. She took it. In her hand too there was a box.

Sunil went into the class-room.

The teacher too carrying the two parcels came there when the bell rang. The children seeing the parcels entered into a quiet discussion. They merely guessed, yet what they contained nobody was able to tell. After a little while the teacher addressed the class.

" Be silent. In our class do you children know who is the first? "

" Yes " all crying out looked at Nimal.

" Who? "

" Nimal "

" Correct, therefore I and another gentleman have bought a present to be given to Nimal. When Nimal takes the present all must clap their hands; do you understand? "

" Yes "

" Nimal " called the teacher.

Nimal slowly went towards her seat.

The teacher handed over the two parcels to Nimal. Nimal took them with both his hands, greeted her by bowing his head and went back.

A great curiosity arose in the children.

" What's it? what's it? " questioned some in their hushed discussion.

" Open and show Nimal " said the class teacher. Nimal opened the bag and took out the shirt and a pair of shorts which were there.

" Clothes " said the children.

He put it back into the bag and opened the other parcel. He took out what was there too.

" New black shoes " said the children.

Nimal who was smiling kept the two parcels aside.

" Now Nimal can come nicely on the day of the prize giving isn't it " asked Sunil when going home that day.

To this Nimal's answer was a happy smile.

Chapter Seventeen

Nelum Bandara's transfer could not be changed. Therefore they were preparing to go to Kandy to reside. Nelum Bandara would be getting a Government bungalow situated round the lake; that was one relief but that would not help them to reduce their expenses.

A few people who heard about Nelum Bandara's transfer were attempting to get Aluth Walauwa on rent. Maha Kumarihami said " Don't give it to anyone other than to a suitable person."

" I don't know about a suitable person but if the rent is suitable I'll give it " said Nelum Bandara.

" Can't do that; if it is not given to a suitable person the prestige of the Walauwa will be damaged and our prestige too will also be damaged " said Maha Kumarihami.

At the end the house was given to a person pleasant in all respects; to the D. R. O. of the province. From this the prestige of the Aluth Walauwa will increase on one side. That was because it will get the name, ' D. R. O. Walauwa '.

The Maha Kumarihami proposed to give the Galwalewatta and the paddy field on a lease.

" Then what about Muthu Banda? " asked Nelum Dandara.

" We cannot look after all those "

" No mother, let them do it the way they are being done now. I will be able to come on Sundays and look after them, can't I?"

Grandmother was not very happy at this decision. But to Muthu Banda it came as a great relief. Not only that; Nelum Bandara decided to give the stone quarry to Muthu Banda for one year without any payment. Even if that were a payment for looking after the property Muthu Banda thought it a great privilege and accepted it.

The teacher came to know from Nimal that Sunil's father would be going to Kandy on a transfer and that Sunil also will be attending a school in Kandy.

" Is it true Sunil that you are going to a school in Kandy?" asked the class teacher.

" Yes " said Sunil and looked down.

All those in the class looked at one another and were silent.

" Sunil, then are you happy to go? " asked the class teacher again. He looked at her face. Then tears started falling.

" No " Sunil spoke but the sound did not come out. Instead he started sobbing.

Nimal who was standing in the other corner of the class looked out. In him too the breath kept falling rapidly. Tears streamed down his two cheeks and fell on the shirt. He turned to a side so that no one could see him.

The teacher now gazed from Sunil to Nimal as if by instinct. Since she was in the front of the class she saw Nimal's stream of tears as well as his agitation. She was not surprised at it.

" I am very happy that a boy in our class is going to a big school " said the teacher happily.

When Nimal heard this his tears dried up. When Sunil goes and studies well and becomes a good person it will be an honour to us.

" You will write letters and so on to us, won't you Sunil?"

" Yes " said Sunil wiping away the tears.

The teacher thought that it was not an occasion to discuss at length about separation. By doing it she thought that Sunil's sadness may increase. Therefore class work began.

The packing of the household goods of Aluth Walauwa for removal to Kandy had been completed. The next day the Nelum family will leave the village in the morning at an auspicious time. At noon and in the night that day they will have to eat seated on mats. They will have to sleep too on mats. That was because the packing of beds, chairs and tables had been completed. That was the last day that Sunil was attending Gemunu Vidyalaya. He did the class work just as on other days. But he himself could not understand what his feelings were. He felt sad to leave Gemunu Vidyalaya. Yet he was happy that he was going to a new school. He loved to stay in Kandy.

But he felt sad to leave Nelumgama. He just happened to look at Nimal. He felt that his chest went empty. He felt an uneasiness in the stomach as when a swing goes up. He felt a sudden gasp as when a new tumbler slips from his hand and breaks. Leaving Nimal and going was a great sorrow for him.

The last period of the class was over. There was only five minutes for the school to close.

" Children be silent " said the school teacher. The students became silent.

" Because today is the last day of the student life of Sunil in this school I am going to give you a treat. All sit down".

The teacher took a bottle of sweets from the almirah. She opened it and distributed the sweets among the children. The children too ate them happily.

" Sunil you must write letters to us " said the teacher.
Sunil who said " Yes " wrote down her address and those of a few friends.

" Ayubowan " wished the children addressing the teacher. She too wished them in reply.

" To Sunil also " said the teacher.

" Ayubowan Sunil " wished the children.

Sunil with tear-filled eyes put his hands together and while trying to smile worshipped them. The children then dispersed.

At the junction close to the bridge Sunil and Nimal were left alone. Without any conversation they walked along. They came up to the quarry. Yet none of them spoke.

" I'm also about to go to the Walauwa; then we'll go Sudu Appo " said Galbanda in a hurry putting on his sarong and banian.

" Nimal worship Sudu Appo and go " said Galbanda.

Sunil who was not able to talk even a word turned towards Nimal and said, " Don't " and nodded his head. Nimal too who remained as if dumb kept the books on the ground, put his hands together bowed down and worshipped him. Sunil seeing this raised his voice and cried out as if he had been hit by someone. Nimal too cried in the same way. Galbanda too took the large handkerchief from his shoulder and covered the tear drops that came out.

The two lorries loaded with the goods of Aluth Walauwa left early in the morning. Galbanda too went in one lorry. He went to look after the goods as well as to get to know the new place.

Palingumenika, Cecelia with the dog Neela got into the other lorry and went off. Sunil too asked for permission to go in a lorry. His request became abortive with one stare from grandmother.

" Grandmother is very bad "

" I am bad and always so " said grandmother and with a smile looked away.

As the auspicious time drew near they got ready for the journey.

" Here is the key Mudalihami. When the D. R. O. comes give it. According to what he says look after the garden and stay" said appachchi and gave him the key. Mudalihami took the handkerchief from around his neck in his hand and took the key with both his hands. He cried so that the toothless gums were visible and saying, " May the gods look after you " raised both his hands and worshipped them.

Mother gave him some money. Grandmother too opened her purse made of rushes, saying, " Take this for betel ", she threw fifty cents towards him. Mudalihami picked it up.

" I feel sorry for Mudalihami " said Maithri akka smiling sarcastically.

" He is deceitful " said grandmother. Sunil was unable to understand the meaning of those discussions. Sunil of course felt genuinely sorry for Mudalihami. Will the D. R. O. Mahattaya look after him well ? Will he give money to him to purchase betel and tobacco? Will he look after him in sickness and sorrow? If Neela was taken why can't they take Mudalihami.

Appachchi kept on looking at the watch and said " The time is correct ".

" Son you yourself must go first " said aththamma. Appachchi agreed. After that all went down. The milk woman came along the main road carrying an empty bottle and from the steps went over to the other side. " I thought she might be even coming here " said grandmother. The party went to the road. Ranmenika and her daughter were standing behind them

Appachchi brought the car to the foot of the row of steps. Sunil sat in the front seat. Ranmenika and Amitha came up to the car and worshipped the three elders. They then wiped their tears away.

" Without feigning to cry be good " said grandmother.

"Tell Muthu Banda that if he doesn't work properly it will be given over to an outsider " she said further.

" No, no, he will work by putting all his effort " said Ranmenika.

" After the confinement is over come that way; you can see the Perahera too " said mother and gave a coin to Amitha.

" We are going " said appachchi and started driving the car. As they turned from the bridge Sunil saw Nimal carrying books with both his hands walking fast to school.

" There is Nimal! " Sunil cried out.

" Appachchi Nimal is there I'll talk to him and go " said Sunil. Appachchi who heard it automatically applied the brakes.

" Now we'll go. Why do you want to stop again as we are leaving at an auspicious time " said grandmother in a gruff voice. Sunil waved his hand to Nimal kneeling on his seat. Seeing this Nimal allowing the books which were in his right hand to drop waved at him. He waved his hand like a railway guard. He waved his hand until Nimal disappeared from the his sight. After that Sunil sat in his seat and looked in front of him.

" If this fellow was left at Galwalegedera there wouldn't have been any problem " said cruel aththamma.

Maithri who heard it too laughed. Because of the sunlight Sunil saw his reflection in the glass. Sunil pulled out the handkerchief quietly from his pocket and wiped secretly the tear drops that came out clouding the eyes.

Chapter Eighteen

The car arrived at the Kandy road in half an hour. The party did not talk much. Maithri was nodding Sunil too reclined and closed his eyes. The elders went along thoughtfully.

The sound of buses, cars, trains and human voices were heard from time to time. The travellers did not show much interest in any of them. Since they did not have a proper sleep the previous day they all went in silence; sometimes dozing and half asleep at times.

" There now it's Kandy " said appachchi and drove the car over the Peradeniya bridge. They all shed their drowsiness and sat straight.

" What's the time putha? " asked the grandmother

" Ten O' clock "

" Then we have come quickly " said the mother.

" How can it be quickly? For forty miles two hours "

" Yes of course " said the mother.

" This is the junction from which we turn to the University" said appachchi and showed it with his right hand.

All looked in that direction.

" Here is the Peradeniya Botanical Gardens " he said and showed it with his left hand.

" We shall go there " said Maithri.

" There will be plenty of time to walk about in them " said appachchi smiling.

The car passed Getambe.

" Where are the houses which were here? " asked the grandmother.

" They were all swept away by the floods. Those people stay at Dangolla now after taking Government houses. This Vihara was the only building which was saved from floods in this area. What has been newly built on this side is a part of it" explained appachchi driving the car slowly.

They were silent again.

" There son the lake, There the Maligawa "

" Sadhu! Sadhu! " said the grandmother and keeping her palms together worshipped in the direction of the Maligawa. The others too followed her.

Appachchi who said " Our house is close to the Maligawa " drove the car a few yards along the Lake Drive and cut into a garden on the left and stopped.

Muthu Banda came down from the house which was in front with a smiling face and then came running towards the car.

" At what time did you come? " asked appachchi from him.

" When we came here it was five "

" Why so long? "

" Don't you know; stopping here and there; drinking coffee and smoking cigarettes "

" You also got a good opportunity " said grandmother

" Why Menike, of course " said Muthu Banda and smiled.
Palingumenika and Ceceilia too came there pleased.

" How, is it good. Bola? " asked grandmother

" Ehei " she said and smiled

" Ah we'll now go into the house " said the mother.

" Remember the Gods and the Buddha and step into the house " said grandmother. The mother too turned towards the Maligawa, kept her hands together and worshipped. The others too did so. Then they entered the house.

" May the Gods help us, may the Buddha grant us refuge " said the grandmother.

Goods were stacked in several places. Only the chairs had been kept in some order.

" I of course do not know how to keep them. I just kept them " said Muthu Banda.

" They can be arranged later " said the mother.

The verandah is long. It's in two parts. One part faces the Maligawa. The other part stood with the front towards the lake Maithri and Sunil went and looked at the lake.

" It's very beautiful brother "

" The water shines isn't it? "

" Yes, Oh what's that in the center of the lake? "

" An island isn't it? "

" Oh yes "

The elders walked about in the house. Apart from the drawing room there were two bedrooms, one office room and one store room. The kitchen had been well constructed.

" This is quite enough " said the grandmother.

" Enough, enough " said mother after looking at appachchi and smiling happily.

" At what time have you got to light the fire in the hearth Ayubowan " asked Muthu Banda.

" At fifteen past eleven. A little milk and a few things have to be brought isn't it Muthu Banda? " asked appachchi taking the purse in to his hands.

" I have prepared them " said Muthu Banda and showed half a bottle of milk, a new earthenware pot and a bundle of firewood. The mother who saw them smiled happily.

" It's because you know these things that we brought you " said the grandmother as a mild hint.

" How small is the bundle of firewood " said Maithri.

" These are what you get here Appo "

The mother went to the kitchen and boiled the milk at the auspicious time. " Ha! now cook something " she said and asked them to take rice and condiments.

A visitor came there; he too was clad like Muthu Banda.

" Who are you? " asked appachchi

" I am the person who looks after the Government bungalows"

" Ha good. Can you find a man for us to get these goods arranged? "

" Why do you need any one? I can " said he.

" Son where is the Kachcheri? " asked the grandmother.

" There it is " said appachchi going towards the edge of the verandah and pointing his finger at it. All looked in that direction in search of it.

" So close " asked the grandmother.

" Yes, yes, that is the Museum. The next is the court house. The next is the Kachcheri. "

" Then I can come home for lunch? "

" After lunch I can sleep also and go " said appachchi very happily.

" Tea is ready " said Muthu Banda.

" Muthu Banda is the chief to day " said grandmother going inside the house. The others too went inside laughing.

" I am the one who came first to reside in the house " said Muthu Banda jokingly.

On the table lay the tea pot, the milk jug and the bottles of sugar. Close by was the basket made out of reeds which was brought in the car. Mother opened it and took out the pieces of milk rice and arranged them on the tray. She said " Eat them as they are ".

All took a piece of milk rice each and ate them looking at the lake.

Sunil remembered Nimal. Only if Nimal too were present!

Chapter Nineteen

The next day in the morning Nelum Bandara went for work in the kachcheri. He got a place in the land office pertaining to work in respect of farmers in the colonies. It was quite different to court work. There was a person in that office who knew Nelum Bandara. He was Ariyadasa. He had worked with Nelum Bandara for some time in court together.

" What Ariye? It is not like in courts. There is no outside benefit here " said Nelum Bandara to Ariyadasa as if for fun

" Have a little patience and see " said Ariyadasa and went away smiling.

Maithri was admitted to Hemantha Vidyalaya. It is situated on the summit of Wewakanda in a very beautiful spot. It is the most prestigious school where girls of good families go to study.

" Expenses are heavy. I don't know what I should do " said Nelum Bandara.

" There is nothing that could be done. When all the children of prestigious families go there how can we send them to another " argued the Maha kumarihami.

Because of Maithri the monthly expenses was more than forty rupees per month. When staying at Nelumpura the expenses on behalf of her was only two rupees. From time to time on account of functions and ceremonies money had to be paid. Yet the monthly expenses had never exceeded more than five rupees.

Sunil was sent to Vasantha Vidyalaya. That was one of the best schools in Kandy. Nelum Bandara made efforts to get Sunil admitted to Sarath Vidyalaya. But because of insufficient room he wasn't able to do so.

" In a way that turned out to be good " said Bandara once to Kumarihami. " For this school too the expenses would be around fifty rupees. Now we get it done for five rupees "

" Then how much is Sarath better than Vasantha? In any school what is taught now is Sinhala, isn't it? "

" But when it is said that he studied in a prestigious school it's an honour isn't it? " put in Loku Kumarihami.

" That was before mother. Now they are all the same " said Bandara.

Maithri and Sunil go to school in the car. Before Nelum Bandara goes to the kachcheri he drops them at school and comes back. In the afternoon they have their food in the respective schools. In the evening Nelum Bandara again goes and comes with the children.

" There is a big problem to me " grumbled Nelum Bandara.

" But that's good for the battery " he says and feels comforted.

The name of the Government bungalow in which the Nelum family lives is called ' Maya '. Two more bungalows called ' Ruhunu ' and ' Pihity ' was in the neighbourhood.

" Why are these bungalows given these names? " asked Nelum Bandara from the keeper of the bungalows.

" Sir, the doors of these bungalows are turned towards those provinces " he answered.

" Right, right good idea isn't it? " asked the Kumarihami with a smile.

" Yes, yes " said the Maha Kumarihami.

The bungalow that was closest to ' Maya ' was ' Ruhunu '. The person who occupied it was a clerk in the kachcheri. His name is Kandalanda. Both Kandalanda and Nelum Bandara could be said to be persons who are alike. Both are almost of the of the same age. They are clerks in the second class. The service of both are similar. Both had a son and a daughter each. Their wives too were similar in age. Their widowed mothers lived with them. Both have two cars. Both had two dogs.

" This is like as if prearranged " said the two Kumarihami's laughing.

The two families of Nelum and Kandalanda quite quickly fell into a close relationship. The two Maha Kumarihamis came to a stage when they could not be without each other. The four children too went to school together. One day they went in Kandalanda's car, the other day in Nelum Bandara's car. But to Sunil there wasn't a friend like Nimal ever.

A week after Sunil came to Kandy he wrote a letter to Nimal.

' Maya '
Lake Road
Kandy.

My dear Nimal,

I am studying at Vasantha Vidyalaya. It's larger than Gemunu. But for me it's still my old school that I like most.

Our house is close to the lake. I remain always at home. I haven't got to walk like at your place. Can't you tell your father and come to this school. If you come here what a fine thing it would be. I conclude by remembering all my friends there.

I remain your friend,
Sunil.

In two days a reply came.

Galwalegedara
Nelumgama
Nelumpura.

My dear Sunil,

Thank you for your letter. I hope you are studying well. If I am able I shall come for a day at least during Perehara time. Your absence is a great loss to me. The help that you gave me, when can I repay you. I was told by the teacher only after you had gone to Kandy that the suit which was given to me by the teacher for the prize giving was from you. When I heard it I felt very sad. I thank you for asking me to come to that school. How do we know when those will happen.

We will pray that we'll be born close to each other in our next life. May you all be happy.

Yours ever loving
Nimal

Sunil read the last part of the letter through his tears.

Chapter Twenty

Galwalegedara Ranmenika's confinement this time was very difficult. She even had to go to the hospital. The child born was also another girl. On account of none of the others did she suffer so much and had to spend so much as for this. Muthu Banda came out with these as a reason for his pain of mind.

" About how much did you spend? " asked Ranmenika, who was sprawling in the camp bed and moaning.

" To the doctor fifteen rupees; for the car six rupees; and the four rupees for the injection was obtained by selling Nimal's pair of shoes " said Muthu Banda.

" My fate; what am I to do! " cried Ranmenika.

" This girl she is a miserable wretch; no milk at all to drink" she said biting her teeth. She looked at the girl and with tears coming down her face anew she kissed her little face.

The money spent for her confinement was obtained by selling the buffalo. If there wasn't a buffalo to work the paddy fields next season it will be a great loss. Therefore one must be purchased quickly.

For a long time Ranmenika remained a sick person. The Gurunnanse who reads horoscopes had said that the little daughter's influence on the parents was exceedingly bad. Ranmenika could not devote herself to any kind of work until four or five months passed by. She was even unable to nurse the little one. Therefore the little one had to be given tinned milk. The time came when Nimal had to be given new books.Not only books, clothes too should be bought. Nimal did not have anything to wear except the suit that was presented to him by Sunil.

" Son is it very necessary for you to study further " asked Muthu Banda from Nimal when it was not possible for him to remain silent.

Thinking that this question would come up some time Nimal waited in expectation of it. This was not because he was hostile towards his father. It was also not because of the wicked suggestions of Maha Kumarihami. It was because he understood the troubles that his mother and father had. It was also because when he is with the other boys as a reason of the clothes he wore he was unable to take a position equal to that of the boys. Although it was a question that he expected tears were hanging in his eyes which were turned towards the floor. Yet he came out with the answer that he had prepared several days ago.

" No appachchi what I have learnt is enough now. I will help you appachchi "

Muthu Banda who saw his two eyes and heard his answers looked away; may be to hide his intense sorrow.

Now Nimal works in the stone quarry. He helps his father in the paddy fields and elsewhere. But he never mentioned this in any of his letters to Sunil. He did not think of writing it.

Chapter Twenty One

One day Muthu Banda received a letter from the Maha Kumarihami. It was mentioned there that he should get one hundred coconuts plucked and husked and that she is coming on Sunday to remove them.

Muthu Banda too as he had been asked arranged and kept them ready. Nelum Bandara and Maha Kumarihami came by car on Sunday. The car was stopped near the stone quarry, Maha Kumarihami called Muthu Banda. She said that she will be coming there to take the coconuts after returning from the D. R. O. Walauwa. Maha Kumarihami saw Nimal who was breaking stones there.

" What, patiya didn't you go to school today? "
Nimal silently looked up and down.

" He does not go to school now " answered Muthu Banda.

" Is it true; from when is it? "

" It's almost a month now "

" Why is that? "

" Since it's not of any use " said Muthu Banda.

" Patiya then come with us to go to Kandy. Muthu Banda, keep that boy ready for us to take. We'll go son " said Maha Kumarihami in one breath.

Nelum Bandara drove the car. Muthu Banda with a hasty and troubled mind remained looking at the car. Nimal stopped his work and looked at the father. The father looked down. Nimal again started breaking stones. Muthu Banda too continued his work. In a moment he put the hammer on the ground and looked at his son.

" Son do you wish to go to Kandy? "

" No "

" Why? "

" It's good here for me "

" If you go then you can play with Sudu Appo "

" If I stay here can't I help appachchi's work? "

" It does not matter. You go to Kandy. Go home and tell your mother and wear something and come "

Nimal looked here and there in wonder.

" When will I come back again appachchi? "

" Come when the Kumarihamis tell you " said Muthu Banda and turned his tear-filled eyes away.

" Is appachchi telling me to go definitely? "

" Yes, go and return; otherwise the Kumarihamis will get angry "

Nimal as if one without any feelings went down from the quarry and went home. The mother was moaning lying down. The sister was cooking rice for the afternoon meal.

" What is it son? "

" I was asked to go to Kandy with the Menikes "

" Who said it? "

" Loku Menike told appachchi. Appachchi asked me to get ready and come "

Then Muthu Banda too came there.

" Did you hear? "

" What? "

" Maha Menike says to send Nimal to Kandy "

" How can you send him! " said Ranmenika moaning and added " Who will break the stones: who will look after the young ones? "

" By saying those it will be of no purpose. That woman told me to get ready and stay. "

" Why didn't you tell that I am still sick "

" By telling those am I to get a scolding. It's not that: let the son go. "

" Then let anything happen. " Ranmenika moaned.

Nimal too, wore the pair of trousers and the shirt given by Sunil and ate the rice served by Amitha.

" Brother are you going to Kandy to stay there? "

" I don't know "

" Why malli, do you not like to go? "

" I am going because appachchi tells me "

" How good it is there! "

Immediately the horn of the car was heard.

" I am coming " said Muthu Banda, and going towards the quarry said, " Son bring your clothes and come." Nimal wrapped up a sarong and a banian with an old newspaper.

" Malli worship mother and go " whispered Amitha to him.

Nimal knelt down before his mother and worshipped her.

The mother kissed Nimal's head saying " May the Gods protect my son "

Kuda Leela too came there asking. " Koda aiya nanne? "

Nimal told her " Nangita theen bola gennan. "

Saying " Matath theen bola " punchi malli too came there.

Nimal kissed the faces of the young ones and taking the hand of kuda nangi and kissing it worshipped the elder sister and wishing them all went away. Muthu Banda put the two gunny bags of coconuts into the boot of the car.

The Maha Kumarihami seeing Nimal coming said, " Ha it may be that you took time in order to wear trousers "

" Sending putha is a great loss for me "

" People sometimes have to bear up big losses than that; if these lands are given on lease to people our profits would be greater than this " said the Maha Kumarihami.

" Get in patiya in front " said the Maha Kumarihami. Nimal went and knelt before Muthu Banda's feet and worshipped him.

" Ha, ha. "

" The boy knows good manners " said Nelum Bandara

" Why not. Boys now are very mature " said Maha Kumarihami.

Nimal sat in the front seat. The car drove off.

" What is your name. boy? " asked the Maha Kumarihami.

" Nimal "

" We can't use that name. from today we will call you 'Nima'"

Chapter Twenty Two

Nimal was going to Kandy for the first time. Before this he tried to go to Kandy several times to see the Perehara. Because of some thing or other he could not.

Therefore as he took an interest in things that he saw and heard he forgot about the past and the future. He thought of asking about what he saw as he went along. But he feared even to open his mouth. Nelum Bandara and his mother went in silence.

As the car stopped at the ' Maya ' garden Sunil came there running. Nimal having tucked the parcel under the arm-pit alighted from the car. Sunil without being able to believe his eyes, with open mouth, with eyes open wide and with partly raised arms shouted "Nimal. "

Nimal with a shy smile looked at Maha Kumarihami, Nelum Bandara and Sunil. Nimal had grown slightly tall and turned a little dark. He was also thin. Maha Kumarihami got down from the car.

" Nimal, did you come to stay here? " asked Sunil taking a hand of his.

Nimal was silent even for that.

" The rigmarole later, go boy from that side to the kitchen" said the Maha Kumarihami and stepped into the house

Nimal too went to the side he was shown.

" Come this way Nimal " said Sunil trying to get his friend to the front verandah.

Nimal who understood Maha Kumarihami's ways said " No, I shall come from this side " and went from the side of the house towards the back verandah. Sunil too followed him.

" Nimal why didn't you put on your shoes and come? " asked Sunil as they went.

" I thought that this is good "

" Did you come solely to stay here? "

" I don't know "

" Who asked you to come? "

" Loku Menike "

" Do you want to go to school here? "

" No "

" Then? "

" I don't know. I was asked to come and I came "

Presently Maha Kumarihami came to the rear verandah saying,

" Sit on that stool ", and showed a low stool to Nimal.

Sunil was displeased with the seat given to Nimal. But without mentioning anything he went towards aththamma and holding her hand he said " Good aththamma "

" Mokada appa. How could I have turned out to be good today. I have never been that before " said Maha Kumarihami smiling.

" Because you brought Nimal "

" Is it that! Then it doesn't matter. But I will tell you one thing. Don't you spoil him now "

" Don't tell him ' pancha ' aththamma, call him Nimal "

" Now this is the other thing. You can't do as you want "

" From today that boy's name is Nima. Keep that well in your mind. "

" Why is that? "

" That is how it is "

At that moment mother came there.

" The boy is good isn't it, to take the food to school? "

" I didn't even see " said mother and looked closely at Nimal and asked " Ha! Is it you? "

Nimal came and worshipped her. Sunil was in deep thought.

" Ha! Sit down will you " said mother and came inside the house and said " The boy is good ", and asked " Isn't it Muthu Banda's boy? "

" Yes "

" Then school? "

" It seems he's not going to school. When I went he was breaking stones. I put him in the car and came away. It's good isn't that so? " asked aththamma with pride.

" Very good mother. Son it's good isn't it? " said mother and winked at aththamma without being seen by Sunil.

" I don't know " said Sunil who was not able to understand anything that was happening correctly. He then went out of the place into the open with an unhappy face.

Sunil walked about the place for a little while and went inside the house again. He then saw Nimal seated in the rear verandah on a stool eating bread from an enamel plate. He was wearing a sarong and a banian. Sunil stood without being seen by his friend and went back again. He sat on a reclining chair in the verandah and looked at the lake and began thinking

The golden rays of the setting sun drifted along the rows of waves. The sprinklers in the island scattered the water around. In the centre of the spreading drops of water colours of the rainbow appeared. A flock of birds came flying from the direction of Gundumale. A flock of crows was drawn towards them. Clouds of various shapes and sizes drifted hither and thither in the sky. One cloud appeared as if Ehelepola Kumarihami was plunging into the lake with a stone tied to her neck.

Sunil's thoughts too were without any beauty or use, without a boundary or an end or depth or measurement but rose upon spontaneously without any effort. Nimal has come to be a servant. From today, his name is not Nimal but ' Nima '. Grandmother calls him 'Pancha '. He has left school; why is this.

Sunil saw Nimal taking an empty gunny bag and going towards the garage. Sunil too went there.

" What is it Nimal? "

" I was asked to take coconuts "

Sunil opened the boot. Nimal pulled out a gunny bag from the boot with coconuts. Sunil helped him. Nimal untied the gunny bag took coconuts out of it and put them into the bag that he brought. He put fifteen into it and carried it. Sunil too helped him. The coconuts were taken into the store room and were heaped up. Later Sunil too brought a gunny bag and both of them took the nuts away.

" Sunil go inside the house. That boy will do that " shouted the grandmother. But he ignored it and helped to carry all the hundred nuts. After all the nuts were carried Nimal went and sat on the stool.

" You cannot remain lazy like that. Bring some manure from that place and put it into the flower beds " ordered aththamma.

Nimal took a basket and a mammoty and went there. Sunil took a basket and brought manure on the sly. Grandmother who saw it scolded Sunil.

Chapter Twenty Three

After it grew dark Sunil went with Nimal towards the verandah.

" Nima, where are you going? " shouted Maha
Kumarihami.

Nimal was startled. " Hereafter you must never go through
the centre of the house. You must go round the house. It is this
son who is spoiling this boy. The parents do not take any notice
of this. The son grows up the way he wants " said the Maha
Kumarihami forcefully and in anger.

The mother who was hurt at this came out with a flushed face
saying " Son if you don't listen to what we say we'll tie you to a
tree and beat you. Leave that boy to do what he is doing. You
read a book"

" It's not for anything else daughter; if you do not bring
up the boy from the first day itself later there will be immense
trouble"

" Yes it's the son who does not allow it " said the mother
too.

Nimal went again to the back and after going round the house
he came to the front. There he met Sunil.

" Come here Nimal! "

" I can't Appo. Loku Menike will scold me. Do not
even talk with me too much " said Nimal.

" It does not matter, come here " said Sunil and holding his hand he went with Nimal to the edge of the verandah and showed him the lake, the maligawa, and other buildings like the kachcheri.

Maithri who had gone to the ' Ruhunu ' bungalow to play came there. She saw the two friends.

" Brother who is this? "

" Sister, you know Nimal don't you? "

She too recognized Nimal. Maithri remembered Nimal who went in the car that day with coconut oil streaming down.

" How do I know him? " she said and went inside the house with an upward jerk of her chin.

" Who is that boy who is with malli holding hands? " asked Maithri looking at both mother and grandmother.

Grandmother groaning, biting her teeth and lips looked from the corner of her eyes at mother. She curled her fingers and made fists out of her hands. Mother got very angry. That was not solely for what Sunil did, but because of grandmother. Mother got up. She took the cane that was at the end of the deer horn which was used to beat the dog.

" Sunil come here"

Sunil heard mother's angry voice and came running towards her. She hit him one blow on his back with the cane.

" If you go to talk with that boy again I will skin you, take care " said the mother and gave him another blow.

" What's this! Can you be without talking? " he started snivelling and then burst out crying loudly. Nimal who saw the punishment that Sunil had to suffer because of him sat in the verandah and shed tears. What is the wrong that Sunil did. Is it a fault to talk to Nimal ? Is Nimal a bad boy?

" Nima, Nima " called the Maha Kumarihami.

" Why " said Nimal.

" Don't say why. When you are called, say 'Enawa' do you understand? " said the grandmother.

Maithri who heard it began laughing " Hei, hei "

" Parippu school isn't it? He is first in the class isn't it." Sunil stared at ' Napuru Maithri ' like a tiger.

" Come here Pancha , here " grandmother said to Nimal who was leaning against the wall of the drawing room.

He came towards her touching the wall.

" The wall will not fall. Don't touch it, it will become dirty. Stand upright. This is Kandy. Not Nelumgama. Did you understand? Well brought up people live here. We must also stay like well brought up people. Do you understand? Did you understand?" asked grandmother twice or thrice.

" Yes " said Nimal.

" Don't say ' how ' ", hereafter when we call you say Ehei "

Maithri started laughing saying " How, how "

" Duwa " said grandmother and silenced her.

Yet she laughed slowly.

" Tell ' Ehei ' did you understand? Look this way Pancha" said aththamma.

Nimal looked at her. Tears stared falling from his eyes.

" Did you hear what I said? " grandmother started asking him.

" I heard " said Nimal.

But why does Nimal say ' Ehei ' Nimal does not belong to the people who say ' Ehei ' to laymen.

" This is Loku Appo " said grandmother pointing at Maithri.

" That is Sudu Appo " she said pointing at Sunil.

" I am not Appo I am Sunil " he said angrily.

" You tell Walauwe Hamuduruwo to me; Appo's mother Dingiri Hamuduruwo. "

" Then the father of both Appo's, Bandara Hamuduruwo"

" I understand " said Nimal. Yet he wondered at the new way of addressing them.

Chapter Twenty Four

Dinner time came. Cecelia came and called Sunil for dinner.

" This afternoon too there may not have been a satisfactory meal. Give Nimal also rice " said grandmother.

Cecelia too accordingly put rice into an enamel plate and gave Nima who was seated on a small stool. Sunil who was seated at the table served himself rice hastily and saying, " I shall eat there" took the plate and attempted to go towards the kitchen.

" Without being childish remain here and eat " rebuked the mother.

" I can't, I shall eat with Nimal " said Sunil too disobediently.

" Bring that cane Cecelia "

" Then I will not eat "

" If you are not eating do nothing "

Sunil kept the plate and tried to go towards the kitchen.

" Don't go there, go out " said the mother taking the cane into her hand and standing against the door of the dining room.

" In this place nothing could be done " said Sunil and coming to the table sat at it muttering while eating the food.

" Only I will not say anything to son now " said grandmother in anger.

Nimal was given the verandah to sleep.

" You don't feel lonely do you? " asked the mother.

" No "

Cecelia brought a ' Thalakola ' mat and an old pillow and gave them to Nimal. Nimal slept in the verandah. Sunil went up to the place where his mother was seated and leaned against her, embraced her neck, looked at her face and smiled a little.

" Please amma allow me to do one thing " Sunil begged her.

" What is it? "

" Shall I too sleep in the verandah? "

" The dew will fall on you and do you want to get a cold? "

" Then Nimal sleeps in the open "

" That boy has got used to it "

" Please amma then I'll tell Nimal to sleep in my room?"

" Go without your jokes. Go and sleep in your bed " said mother and pushed him.

" Cecelia did you cover putha's bed with a new cloth? "

" Ehei "

Maha Kumarihami saw Nimal sleeping with bent body. His legs had been taken inside the sarong, his two arms tucked under the chin.

" Cecelia bring putha's old blanket and give it to Nima"

" Nima, are you feeling cold, boy? "

" Ow; Ehei "

Sunil who heard it opened the door of the wardrobe and brought his old blanket and gave it to Nimal. He took it and covering himself well, slept enjoying the soft breeze blowing towards the lake. Sunil looked at him for a little while and staring at his mother went inside the house. The Maha Kumarihami too came out to chew some betel.

" Why did you give that good blanket? " she said with a displeased face.

" Here it is colder than at Nelumpura " said mother

" When you get accustomed to things that you are not accustomed to it's troublesome to you in the future " said grandmother further.

Nimal who heard it thought of throwing it away. After the two women went inside the house chewing betel Nimal slept in comfort.

How much better it is here than sleeping in the hut near the stone quarry, on the clay floor and on the torn old mat thought Nimal. But that was Nimal's house; isn't it. But how can an outside place be better than one's own. Sunil too started thinking. It's sin for Nimal.

Sunil while sleeping in a warm room, on a warm bed, on a warm mattress, on a new bed spread, covering himself with a new blanket but Nimal the first in his class was sleeping on the floor in the cold. He felt very sad.

Later in the night it began to rain and because of the strong winds the verandah was becoming wet. Nimal was soaked and he moved his mat and pillow close to the wall and attempted to sleep. However, the rain and wind increased and Nimal found it impossible to do so. He rolled up his wet mat and sat leaning against the wall.

Sunil hearing the movements outside awoke and climbed down from his bed. He peeped through the keyhole and saw Nimal. Sunil unlocked the door and opened it, and hearing this noise Nimal looked and saw Sunil. Sunil called out to Nimal in a low voice.

" Nimal "

" Yes " replied Nimal.

" You are getting wet. Come inside "

Nimal hesitated.

" Walauwe Hamuduruwo will scold " he said.

" Aththamma is asleep. Come in quickly " Sunil said and collecting Nimal's mat and pillow carried them into the room and closed the door.

Sunil asked Nimal to share the bed but Nimal refused. Sunil tried to force him but Nimal resisted and unrolled the mat and slept on the floor. Sunil too spread a sheet on the floor and slept.

Sunil's mother awoke at the sound of the heavy rain and carrying a basin went to the verandah to leave it were the roof was leaking. She then looked into Sunil's room and was startled to see the bed empty. She looked about and saw the two boys sleeping on the ground. She carried Sunil who was fast asleep, and placed him on the bed. She bent down close to Nimal and covered him with a sheet.

Nimal turned over on his right side and muttered in his sleep " Ha Ha Ha. Sleep my little sister ".

Chapter Twenty Five

On Monday morning the ' Maya ' girl and the ' Ruhunu ' girl
went to school in Nelum Bandara's car. Nimal too went with
them. This was to find out the road in order to take the food.
First they went to Hemantha girls school. Nelum Bandara went
with Nimal and showed him the room where children eat. The
two girls got down from the car and went towards their class
rooms.

    " Get down from the bus at that place and go along the
row of steps; keep the food tray in this room and come. Did you
understand? "

    " Ehei "

    " In the evening when I come the tray could be taken
home; did you hear? "

    " Ehei "

Then they went to Vasantha Vidyalaya. There too Nimal was
shown the room where the food was kept. Nimal learnt his work
quickly. He saw the boutique where they buy goods, the veg-
etable shop, the newspaper stall, the place where milk is bought,
the laundry and everything about them. Nimal always tried to
do his work well. But it was rarely that he got a good name.
Specially Maha Kumarihami always called him with a hint, a
scolding, with a stare and often with a knock. Nimal was not
much accustomed to hints, scoldings and beatings. Even in
school he did his school work well and on time.

At home too before his mother or father reminded him twice he did it. Here too Nimal tried to do whatever is given to him very well and without a waste of time. Here too he learnt the new way of addressing people quickly and used it. But Maha Kumarihami was not quite satisfied. She always spoke to him antagonistically. Apart from Nimal she did not call him even Nima. She always called him either 'Pancha' or ' Kolla '.

Nelum Bandara and Kumarihami were not so cruel. Yet both of them appeared to be in fear of Maha Kumarihami. In everything they were forced to obey her. Because of Maithri Nimal suffered great pain of mind. She was always a tale carrier. If Nimal talked to Sunil, or played with him, or went for a walk in the garden with him or did anything whatsoever she will even make up a story or tell something to the Maha Kumarihami and get both of them scolded. There was some wrong alleged to have been done daily by Nimal in taking the food to school.

What dirt is smeared on the tray that Nima brings. I can't bear it... Nima came today very late... I saw Nima talking to another boy and coming... See aththamma this Nima plucked flowers from the school flower tree... Maithri has some allegation to be made everyday. Yet Nimal is not spiteful towards Maithri. He does not get angry even if she scolds him. Whatever she says or does he bears up with a smile. He likes her.

The biggest worry that Nimal cannot bear up is Sunil's intense kindness. There is nothing else on earth more pleasant than seeing his face, hearing his talk, and having his association. When Nimal remembers his home the huge fire of sorrow that rises is only quelled by remembering Sunil.

Nimal remembered the drops of perspiration trickling down the scarred forehead of his father, and his mother lying on the camp bed groaning and scolding the little ones. Nimal remembers his little sister seated near mother and babbling with the cadjans of the roof.

He remembers the two little brothers and two little sisters who follow him morning and evening asking for lozenges. He remembers Amitha akka who talks in a mature language about the difficulties of the family. Then almost a heart rending sorrow arises in him. A sorrow that makes him fly homewards arises in him. But all those sorrows are lightened by thinking of Sunil.

Nimal suffers great pain of mind since Sunil endures hardships as a reason of Nimal. If Sunil is seen talking to Nimal, playing with Nimal, sitting with Nimal on the floor, Maha Kumarihami is displeased. If an incident similar to any of these take place she reprimands Sunil. Nimal too attempts to keep away as far as possible from Sunil. But whenever Sunil gets an opportunity he comes close to Nimal. They spend their time very happily when Nimal comes to Vasantha Vidyalaya with the food. Sunil goes with Nimal to a corner far away in the playground and talks about all sorts of things.

Sunil tells Nimal everything that happens at school. He tells him even about his class work. Therefore Nimal is like a boy studying in Sunil's class. He knows almost everything.

Chapter Twenty Six

It was a dark day. That morning Nimal awoke late.

" What boy! Until the sun shines on your back you are asleep? " said Maha Kumarihami and coming into the verandah she knocked his side with her foot. That whole day was wretched. The milk bottle given by the milkman was broken. Maha Kumarihami scolded Nimal profusely. She gave him a knock too. She threatened not to give him tea. Sunil who opposed these also received a blow from the cane.

Nimal who carried the two food trays fell down as he climbed the bus. Although he was not injured the food got scattered all over. Therefore he went back and told them what happened. The Maha Kumarihami invoked the wrath of all the Gods. She ground her remaining teeth stumps noisily and went about the house cackling like a hen bitten by black ants. The Kumarihami also abused him much and prepared the food to be taken again.

The large water jug that was kept on the table fell from Nimal's hands on the floor of the room where the water was and broke into bits; Nimal wept like a child.

" That was done by him intentionally... done intentionally " said Maha Kumarihami and holding him by both his hands she went on hitting him with a knotty stick. Nimal cried aloud. Sunil ran to the spot and took the stick by force from her and broke it into three or four pieces. He then put them into the hearth. Maha Kumarihami saw this and began shedding her tears like a girl and lay on the bed and cried uttering lamentations.

Nelum Bandara asked the reason why Maha Kumarihami was lamenting; when he heard the reasons he lost his temper like a cobra. He took the cane, called Sunil and without asking him anything began hitting him. He beat him like a madman. Sunil summoned all his strength and cried while jumping up and down.

" Please appachchi never again appachchi " shouted Sunil. Nimal too ran there and said, " Please Bandara Hamuduruwo don't hit appo ". He tried to stand between Sunil and the father. A few blows struck Nimal. Nelum Bandara also hit him several times. Since he seldom gets angry and since Kumarihami knows it she jumped in front of him and held her husband's hand and stopped it. Nelum Bandara without letting hold of the cane said, " Go and worship grandmother and come"

After that Nelum Bandara threw the cane away and without talking went to the verandah, sat on a chair, lit a cigarette and wiped both his eyes.

Chapter Twenty Seven

That night ' Maya ' bungalow looked an abandoned house. No one spoke much. All ate the food silently. No one spoke more than what was necessary. Sunil who still wept ate one or two mouthfuls and went to bed. The mother went there and applied coconut oil on the marks. Maha Kumarihami ate alone after all the others had eaten. Only the daughter-in-law was seated by the corner of the table engaged in stitching some thing in order to drive away her loneliness.

That night too there was heavy rain. It rained harder than on the day Nimal came to Kandy. It rained amidst thunder and lightning. The sound of the wind was frightening. The sound of the storm was spreading as if Gundumale was rooted out and was drifting towards Udawatta. It was not only the floor of the verandah that got wet; even the walls were getting wet. Apart from Nimal being unable to sleep there was no room even for him to stand.

The clock struck two. The rain did not cease yet. Nimal covered himself from head to foot and wrapped the mat round his waist and leaned against the wall. The door of Sunil's room opened

  " Nimal come inside "

  " I can't Appo I'll stay here "

  " Come here " said Sunil and pulled him towards the room. Nimal too agreed half heartedly. Sunil took his friend inside and locked the door. That day Sunil did not call Nimal to his bed. It was because Nimal would never have agreed to it Similarly Sunil did not come down from the bed. That too was because Nimal would not have liked it. As a reason of the pain of cane marks they were unable to sleep comfortably.

" Are there cane marks on you too? " asked Sunil in a low voice. Nimal said " It pains a little here " and raised the sarong. Sunil, in the night took the lamp and examined Nimal One spot at the back of Nimal's thigh had cracked. Sunil applied coconut oil on the spot.

In a moment both were asleep. Maha Kumarihami awoke because of the rain. She took the torch and examined the leaks in the living room. In two places, a basin and a basket had been kept. She thought it was by the daughter-in-law. Then Maha Kumarihami went into Sunil's room and examined it. She saw Nimal sleeping there. She was stupefied. As if she were under a spell she took breaths in quick succession. How obstinate is Sunil. However much anyone tells him he does what he likes Nima too suits him. His cheek!. Covering himself with a blanket how he sleeps with pride! She thought of pouring the rain water collected in the basin on Nimal's face. But with great difficulty she suppressed the thought. She went up to the place where Nimal was sleeping and kicked his side with her foot Nimal awoke and looked at her. Maha Kumarihami bent towards him and abused him under her breath

" Get up you boy "

Nimal got up.

" Take the mat and the pillow "

Nimal took them.

" Go out " she opened the door Nimal went out. The

blowing of the wind reached the room. Sunil groaned, turned the other side and slept.

" Pleasant sleep for this fellow - Gampaluwa " said the old lady. After she put her head out and abused Nimal she went inside and closed the door. She took the key and went to her room.

Chapter Twenty Eight

" Cecelia! Cecelia! " called the Maha Kumarihami early in the morning lying in her bed.

" Walauwe Hamuduruwo "

" Is that boy Nima still asleep? "

" Still he did not come towards the kitchen " said Cecelia.

" I want to teach him a good lesson today " she said and got down from the bed and taking the bucket of rain water from the drawing room went slowly towards the verandah. Nimal was not there. The mat and the pillow were lying on the floor against the wall.

Saying " Where is this fellow ' bola '.he is not here " she took the bucket of water and went into the kitchen with frustrated hopes.

" He did not come here also " said Palingumenika filling water from the tea pot with the steaming kettle.

" Call him ' bola ' to see "

Cecelia called Nimal. " Nima...Nima...Nima...Nima... "

There was no answer. Because of the turmoil all awoke. They all looked for Nimal everywhere.

" Since the verandah was getting wet we do not know whether he is sleeping somewhere else "

Although Sunil opened his mouth to tell that he got Nimal to come into his room he did not do so. Maha Kumarihami saw Sunil's confusion. She too kept the fact of chasing out Nimal who was sleeping in Sunil's room a secret. If that came to light she thought that her son and daughter- in- law would blame her. They went to 'Ruhunu' bungalow and asked. Nimal had not gone there.

" That fellow would have gone somewhere. What can we do? " said Nelum Bandara in a conciliatory tone.

Yet everybody's anxiety was not reduced.

" Nima has runaway to the jungle. Nima has runaway to the jungle " said Maithri drinking the cup of tea and smiling.

Sunil's eyes had turned red, the mouth twisted and the lips blubbered; the mouth and throat went dry.

" Actually, could anything have happened to Nima? " the Kumarihami asked her husband in a low voice.

" That fellow may have gone somewhere. He cannot escape from amma " said Nelum Bandara in a hush hush tone.

Sunil went to his bed and cried covering his face with a blanket.

" He must be tied to a tree and beaten; because he ran away" said Maha Kumarihami.

" Before he is tied to a tree and beaten he must be found" said Nelum Bandara in an unpleasant tone.

" He couldn't have died; he must have gone somewhere" said Maha Kumarihami shivering. She was frightened thinking that some thing may have happened to Nimal.

Sunil cried without washing his face and without drinking his tea. He refused to go to school.

" How is son? " asked Nelum Bandara from his wife

" When you get angry you don't hit like that! "

" That was not the way I thought of beating him. why? "

" Nothing much; cane marks have not disappeared yet"
The husband and wife decided not to send Sunil that day to school.

" Now what are we going to do about Nimal kolla? "

" I'll go and inform the police. Then I 'll send a tele-gram to Muthu Banda stating that he had runaway. "

" Not telegrams. a post card is enough "

Chapter Twenty Nine

That night in which the Nelum Bandara family was seated for dinner somebody came to the rear verandah and spoke.

" Menike "

" Who is that? " asked Kumarihami.

Palingumenika came running and said, " Muthu Banda has come with Nimal. "

" Nimal " asked Sunil getting up from his seat. He looked at the faces of the elders and sat down again.

The elders too looked at one another's faces.

" Muthu Banda come here will you " ordered Nelum Bandara.

Muthu Banda came there accordingly.

" Why so late in the evening? "

" Our boy came home suddenly. We got frightened. When we asked him why, he said that he saw a dream and that he came. We asked him whether he told you but he said ' No '. Therefore hastily I brought him " explained Muthu Banda.

" Where is the boy? " asked Nelum Bandara.

" There, I brought him. I got frightened thinking that I too will be blamed. " said Muthu Banda looking at Maha Kumarihami and scratching his head and smiling.

" The boy is very obstinate, Galbanda " said Loku Kumarihami.

The husband and wife looked at each other and smiled slightly.

" That sort of thing is not there when he is at home. It may be so when he is out of home " said Muthu Banda.

" I can of course curb his stubbornness but how can I..." said the Maha Kumarihami in anger.

" Give him a beating and bring him up Menike; there is no hindrance from us " said Muthu Banda.

" To beat him and bring him up ... who is he to us; I am thinking just now why should we keep fellows like that " said Maha Kumarihami again as if she were not happy.

" Bring him up in any manner you like and keep him as long as he lives; I nor his mother will utter a word " said Muthu Banda.

Muthu Banda knows quite well the sufferings that his son undergoes. But his only fear is whether they will be chased out of the Galwale property. Therefore Muthu Banda does not like to get angry with the Nelum family at all.

" Please son if you love our family even a little, stay there whatever suffering you undergo " begged Muthu Banda and Ranmenika that morning at the Galwale house. It is after that, that Nimal's tears dried up. It was also after that he realized the importance of his job and also agreed to return.

Everyone at Nelumpura knows that Maha Kumarihami is a heartless and revengeful woman. All the properties have been written in her favour. Since the son is a government servant, before property is written either in his favour or in favour of the daughter- in-law permission should be first obtained from the government. There the question of how such an amount of money came in to their hands arises. Therefore in order to free themselves from the law the Galwale property was written in favour of Maha Kumarihami. Therefore Maha Kumarihami's good disposition towards Muthu Banda is essential.

" If not we may have to beg in the streets " said Muthu
Banda that morning explaining matters to his wife and Nimal.

After dinner the elders sat in the verandah and chewed betel.
According to the advice given by Muthu Banda Nimal came
there and worshipped the three elders.

" I intend to go in the night bus... " said Muthu Banda
amidst all these matters.

" Why so urgent? Stay the night and go " said Nelum
Bandara.

" Aney Aubowan, the problems I have. There is no one
in the house. That woman is still sick... seven children "

" Give them to wherever you can " said Maha
Kumarihami.

" That too I can't even if we all die in a heap " said
Muthu Banda wiping his eyes.

" Then of course what's to be done! Did you chew a
'vita'?" asked Maha Kumarihami.

" Yes " said Muthu Banda. " Then I will take leave of
you" he said and worshipped all three of them saying " Son now
you must stay and be good. Don't run away from here and
don't come there; keep that well in your mind now "

Nimal came forward, went down on his knees before Muthu
Banda's feet and worshipped him. Sunil gazed at this with pro-
found sorrow.

" Here... for the bus at least " said Kumarihami having
brought two rupees and forcing it on him.

" Mata Avasara " he said and scratched his head with
the right hand and bowing looked at them all and went away.

All were pleased in their inner mind at the manner in which the incident came to an end that day. In the same way all decided to treat Nimal with kindness subsequently. Since Muthu Banda gave over Nimal completely and went they thought that they would be able to look after him in the way that they wanted This brought them immense comfort

Chapter Thirty

Soon the office of the Kachcheri Mudliyar would become vacant. This was because the old Mudliyar was going on retirement. Although that post is not so prestigious as before it serves as a rung to go up in the service. Since the Kachcheri Mudliyar goes about with the Government Agent, the post of Kachcheri Mudliyar receives a certain honour. There are rumors to the effect that the post has an abundance of outside favour.

Both Nelum Bandara and Kandalanda were eyeing for the post of Kachcheri Mudliyar. All say that they both have similar qualifications. " Remain where you are " said Ariyadasa to Nelum Bandara. Nelum Bandara also thought whether he should take the advise. The expenses of the family were very high now. It had risen to almost twice the amount than what it was when they were at Nelumpura. Without getting into debt he remains free as a reason of the benefits that he gets from colony work. Although at the beginning there were no such things according to what Ariyadasa said as time passed he managed to organize ways and means to get them. Ariyadasa too greatly helped him. When the colonists in order to build their houses come to the kachcheri to get the money given by the Government Nelum Bandara receives ten percent of the money due on vouchers. Only Ariyadasa knows the manner in which he gets it. Ariyadasa himself gets two percent out of it.

When the colonists come to the kachcheri they make it a practice to come to ' Maya ' bungalow too. Because it is situated near the kachcheri it is very convenient to those who visit it. When they come they bring bees honey, deer flesh, sesame, meneri, kurrakkan, vegetables, eggs, oranges and plantains.

On the day before the vouchers are taken from the kachcheri they come when it is dark in the evening, keep the presents at 'Maya' bungalow and go to the Maligawa. They worship and make offerings at the Maligawa and get to some place and sleep and go to the kachcheri the following day.

The farmers do not regret what is given to the kachcheri Unnanse. "Out of the money given almost free to us by the Government what's the harm if a little is given out. The other thing is that without loafing about we get our work done isn't it ", say the farmers and they are quite pleased. These payments are what should be given, thought some of them.

As a kachcheri Mudliyar, benefits of that nature cannot be thought of. But from the day that Maha Kumarihami heard of the vacancy she said with determination that it must be somehow obtained. The wife too was pleased at the idea. They thought about it more because if Kandalanda gets the post they will become more proud. "It's not the pride but because I will lose the ' Thuttu Deka ' " said Nelum Bandara to the mother and the wife.

" If it's to get something, wherever you are you will get it "

" That's nothing son but it's the honour we will get "

" Apart from everything if they get this too they will do wonders "

Kandalanda and Nelum Bandara therefore became the contestants for the post of Kachcheri Mudliyar. The Nelum family and the Kandalanda family were well disposed towards each other. They moved very closely. They visited each other and exchanged food and drink But everything was done by turns They do these things to show that they are superior to the other They do not do it in public But inwardly they are jealous of each other.

At the kachcheri Kandalanda does Excise work. That too has benefits. Many come to meet him at the ' Ruhunu ' bungalow Most of them come in cars. Some are distinguished people. mudalalis. Sinhala, Malay. Indian and Muslim mudalalis.

To ' Maya ' bungalow come people in rags. poor. lean farmers walking. But to Ruhunu come well dressed people. fat and plump people in cars. About this the Kandalanda people and Nelum people have often laughed.

One evening Maha Kumarihami came out hastily from 'Ruhunu' bungalow and sat heavily on a chair in the verandah Her face had turned red; she was also panting.

" What is it mother? " asked Nelum Bandara.

" How could Ehelepola Adigar be related to Kandalanda people! We are the only people who directly come from them "

" So "

" It's that old woman's boastful talk "

" What is it? "

" That woman says that they are the direct descendants of the legal wife of the father of Ehelepola Adigar. If there is any one else it is from another Kumarihami. Look at their mouths will you "

" What did you say mother? " asked the son looking impatient.

" I told her that the Tamil man called Rama who came to hide the toddy pot at Kandalanda is your great grandfather. "

The husband and wife looked at each other in silence. After this incident ' Ruhunu ' and ' Maya ' drifted apart.

Chapter Thirty One

Another incident took place which widened the estrangement of the two families. It was the annual concert of Vasantha Vidyalaya. The Nelum family went to see it. They were allocated five seats in the first row. They sat in them.

After a little while a teacher came and spoke to Nelum Bandara and requested them to go to the next row.

Nelum Bandara asked why.

" Mr. Kandalanda had booked them " said the teacher kindly.

Maha Kumarihami looked around. The Kandalandas were standing near the door. Kandalanda Maha Kumarihami looked at them as if in ridicule. She didn't like the look.

" We are now seated please tell them to sit behind " said Maha Kumarihami to the teacher.

" That cannot be done. The seats that bear these numbers have been reserved by them. The seats that bear your numbers are behind " said the teacher.

" Then why did you make us sit here? " argued Maha Kumarihami.

" I'm sorry for it. I was not here. Nothing can be done now please go to the back row " said the teacher kindly and firmly.

" Then we shall go home " said Maha Kumarihami.

" Why the back seats are equally good, aren't they ? "

" Then without making us get up tell them to sit down there"

" That I can't tell "

" Then we are going home "

" That is your wish " said the teacher.

" We'll get back and sit " Nelum Bandara proposed.

" Anyone who wants to go to the back may go: I go forwards ", said Maha Kumarihami and walked out. The other two followed her.

The Kandalanda Maha Kumarihami also went with a joyful smile and wiped the seat which Nelum Kumarihami occupied and sat in it. The others of the Kandalanda family also occupied their seats.

To send Sunil to Vasantha Vidyalaya further was a thing that could not be done. Therefore the elders unanimously decided to take him out of the school. Another reason that contributed to it was that the teacher who refused to give the seats. they came to know, was a relative of Kandalanda.

Although the unfortunate incident did not take place as a reason of his fault the principal sent him a letter asking for pardon Yet the decision to remove Sunil did not change. The next question was choosing another school.

A vacancy did not yet occur at Sarath Vidyalaya. At the end they arrived at a decision. It was to send Sunil to Tissa Vidyalaya which is Nelum Bandara's old Vidyalaya. This was because with Nimal's association Sunil will get spoilt and boarding life will be of great use to a boy and further that somehow he might get a place in his old school. The elders confirmed the decision to send Sunil there

Chapter Thirty Two.

Nelum Bandara was appointed as the Kachcheri Mudliyar The happiness of the Nelum family knew no bounds. Maha Kumarihami cried laughed and danced. " Their faces have become small " said Maha Kumarihami referring to the Kandalanda people.

The following evening a party was held for his kachcheri friends at the ' Maya ' bungalow. A large number of people took part in it. Kandalanda too came along. He went back a little later. The wife did not come; " it's like kissing the arm that you can't cut " said Maha Kumarihami to the daughter - in - law smiling." In a way the fact that he came is immensely good? " said the daughter - in -law.

" So son when are we going into the Mudliyar's bungalow?" asked the Maha Kumarihami.

There is a separate bungalow for the Kachcheri Mudliyar It's large and it has a garden. It also has a distinctive look.

" We can go to it; we can also remain here " said Mudliyar Nelum Bandara.

" Why don't we go? Why do we want to creep in with the Kandalanda "

" We shall see towards the end of the month " said Nelum Bandara also.

" Nima come here. now you must call Mudiyanse Hamuduruwo to Bandara Hamuduruwo. what is it? "

" Mudiyanse Hamuduruwo "

" Good, go to the back "

A rumour spread about the kachcheri Mudliyar's appoint-
ment. It was Kandalanda who was to be appointed. Two days
before the appointment a petition was sent against him. The
Government Agent investigated about this and appointed Nelum
Bandara. That rumour could be accepted as true because
Kandalanda was transferred by the Government Agent himself
from his excise work to the room in the land department where
Nelum Bandara worked.

Nelum Bandara and his wife prepared what was needed for
the Mudliyar's bungalow. A new stock of articles was to be
purchased for the drawing room. Old furniture was repaired.
New curtains were stitched. In order to make the bungalow
beautiful little things were purchased whenever they happened
to go to town. Pads of letter heads too were printed.

The day when Sunil had to attend Tissa Vidyalaya came closer
To a letter sent by appachchi to Tissa Vidyalaya appachchi
received a reply. Although there was no room, since the request
by an old boy of the school cannot be ignored a place in the
school boarding had been set apart for little Sunil. A list of
clothes and other requirements had been sent. These too had to
be prepared. Six new white suits were stitched. Four bed spreads
and two sheets, two pairs of shoes; one brown and one black, a
pair of sandals and one large new steel box had to be purchased

Nelum Bandara and the wife had discussed often about these
excessive expenses. Yet the Maha Kumarihami never expressed
any fear or doubt about them. Sunil did not at all wish to attend
a school in the capital. Now he spends all his time shedding
tears. He had told his mother about his displeasure several times

" Please amma I will remain in this same school "

" It's a great thing to go to a big school, son. When you grow big you can get a good job isn't it. " she answered.

Sunil looked for a good time and approached his grandmother

" Please my good grandmother I will go to school from home? "

" Yes, to loaf about with Nima kolla " she said staring.

Sunil went to appachchi too. He went close to where he was reclining and stood there without talking.

" What is it, son? "

" Please appachchi. I can't go leaving home " he said and burst out crying.

" Come here you rogue " said appachchi pulling him by the hand. He kept him on his lap and attempted to pacify him. " We are putting you to a big school for your benefit Appachchi also learnt in it. The teachers and the others there will treat you well. The other thing is that when a boy stays in a boarding he is being brought up well; to learn good things and be of good behaviour. We will come once a month to see you When you feel like phoning us you can do so. "

" How is that? " asked Sunil amidst his tears.

" Why the bungalow to which we are going now has a telephone. "

" Please appachchi. it's good here " said Sunil and re-newed his crying.

" Go, go and sleep without crying. There are two or three days to go isn't it. When you begin crying now itself how can you cry then " said grandmother coming there.

It is not home. or the parents or the grandmother or the sister Maithri that he cannot leave but it is Nimal

Ah Nimal! When he remembers his heart aches. He feels that his stomach is empty. Without any effort he starts sobbing.

Can I go with Nimal? Will there not be enough room to keep him there? If the boarding is large won't they give permission to keep another boy?

" Mother " spoke Sunil lying sprawled on the bed.

" Why son? " asked the mother seated with the grandmother in the living room.

" Will I be able to stay there alone? "

" Why there are about a thousand boys like you "

" But no one knows me "

" When a day or two passes away they'll become friends" The grandmother lighting up her face with a slight smile told the daughter-in-law something or other without being heard.

" Son "

" Why mother? "

" Then am I to send Nimal because you are lonely? "

" Can you do it? "

" Yes " said the mother suppressing her laugh.

" You can? "

Nimal who was lying on a mat in the verandah and listening to this conversation stood up on the mat as if he had got new life.

" Am I to send Nimal with you? " asked the mother again.

" If you can it's good ". As he said this the mother and aththamma laughed. Sunil who heard this knowing that they played a trick on him cried out aloud. Nimal again lay down on the mat.

Chapter Thirty Three

Sunil and Nimal have two tills. They have been kept in Sunil's iron box. When they receive some money they put it in the tills. The elders know that they have money tills. But Maha Kumarihami does not know where Nimal's till has been kept. If she knows where Nimal's till has been kept she will not give permission to allow Nimal's till to be given a high place. But Kumarihami knows it.

Sunil dressed up to go to school. He has to go to Vasantha Vidyalaya only that day and the next; Thursday and Friday From next Monday he will go to Tissa Vidyalaya.

Nimal seeing an opportunity went in to Sunil's room. He spoke to him in a soft voice.

" Sudu Appo please give me my till. "

" Why, is it to put money? "

" No, to take from it. "

" Why? "

" To buy something "

" What? "

" When I bring food I'll tell you. Don't tell anybody "

Sunil gave Nimal's till to him. Sunil started thinking. Before this Nimal has never taken money from the till. When he wants to put some money into it he gives the money to Sunil. Then Sunil puts the money into it. The elders who know that Sunil has a till gives him money to be put into the till. He gets, unlike

Nimal who gets a cent or two, more money like fifty cents, one rupee. When he gets more he puts half into Nimal's till.

What is Nimal going to buy? Good, during meal time he will be able to see it. Sunil wanted to purchase what Nimal is buying. Therefore Sunil put the till too into the school bag when he went to school that day.

Until meal time came Sunil was impatient. Unlike on other days the clock, he thought was going very slowly. At last the clock struck twelve. Sunil went out immediately the class was over. As usual Nimal was there. He was in clean clothes. He always dresses well. But that day he was different and attractive.

" Did you buy that thing? " Sunil asked Nimal while they were going to the play ground.

" Not yet "

" How much money was there? "

" Twenty Seven Rupees and Thirty Two cents "

" What is it Nimal that you are going to buy? "

Nimal looked down at the ground. Then he sat on the play ground. Sunil too sat down. No one else was there.

" What is it Nimal? " asked Sunil and holding Nimal's chin by the hand he raised his face.

Tears flowed from Nimal's two eyes.

" Tell Nimal, tell " asked Sunil in wonder.

Nimal sobbed and cried.

" Nimal please tell, will you. I 'm now angry " said Sunil and wiped his eyes.

Nimal opened his mouth but the voice did not come out. He attempted to speak again.

" I can't stay here without Appo " he said loudly.

A friend of Sunil who heard this as he went along the road, asked "What is it Sunil?" Sunil nodded his head and made him understand that there is no reason to get worried. The friend went away. Sunil and Nimal became silent. In a moment Nimal spoke again.

" Therefore I'm going from here "

" Where? " asked Sunil through tears.

" Somewhere, I'm not going home again "

"Why? "

" If I go home appachchi and the others will be chased out"

" By whom? "

" Loku Menike "

Sunil did not understand the reason. Yet he did not wish to ask him more about it.

" Then where are you going? "

" I am going to Colombo " said Nimal wiping his tears away with great determination.

" How? "

" By train "

" How much is it for the ticket? "

" A man told me that it will be about four rupees"

" After you go to Colombo what will you do? "

" Then, I will find out Appo's Tissa Vidyalaya and come there."

" Don't Nimal; Colombo is very big. There are many roads. You might not be able to find out the school "

" I will somehow find it "

The lunch bell rang and the children went for lunch.

" Come Sunil! Come Sunil! " several shouted

" At what time is the train? " asked Sunil

" Two "

" Sunil come soon " shouted the teacher in charge of the refectory.

Sunil went towards the refectory looking at Nimal.

" I'm going Appo, don't tell anyone " said Nimal as he put his hands together and worshipped him.

Sunil turned back, worshipped Nimal and ran towards the refectory. Sunil was unable either to think anything or say anything. As if in a dream he ran towards the refectory

Chapter Thirty Four

Nimal went slowly towards the Kandy Railway station. He looked back for no reason. He thought he saw Mudiyanse Hamuduruwo's car coming . He got to a side and looked. It was not that car but one of that kind. What Nimal thought was that Sunil had disclosed the secret and sent Nelum Bandara there " No, No " Sunil would never think of anything bad against Nimal. He would never do anything bad to him.

Nimal went in to the Railway station and purchased a third class ticket and entered a compartment. He sat down facing the direction of Colombo. He did not look around but straight ahead He was silent and did not move about. He was thoughtful, in fear and was suspicious. Gradually the compartment became full. An old woman sat down in front of him; a girl was seated close by. Nimal received some sort of cover from them. Some would have thought that they were from one family.

The big bell rang. Immediately the train whistled. The engine sounded and the train moved. " To Colombo sos...sos. " Now of course there was no reason for Nimal to get frightened. There was no way of getting caught. He gave a sigh of relief. He looked here and there a little. There was no one there who knew him. Nimal took out the money hidden in the waist and counted twenty rupees. He tied the money in a small handkerchief and put it under the vest and kept the balance money in the waist itself

Nimal felt hungry. He had not eaten in the afternoon. Every day he had to eat after the food has been delivered to the schools and when he comes back home.

At Peradeniya junction Nimal bought a bun and a banana. When the train resumed the journey he quietly ate them. The hunger was appeased to a great extent. But he felt very thirsty. To bear up the thirst was more difficult than the hunger.

Nimal remembered the stream of cool water that flowed past the quarry in the village. It brought to his mind his father. After that his mother and his brothers and sisters. He remembered Sunil too.

Sunil will be still at school. School closes at three thirty. The car goes there after four thirty. Now they would have come to know that Nimal has run away? What would Maha Kumarihami do? Last time it seems they informed the Police and sent a postcard to appachchi. This time too will they do it? What would appachchi think?

The speed of the train was reduced. Then it stopped. That is at Kadugannawa Railway station. Nimal bought a glass of tea and drank it. Then he sat down. Now of course he felt fine The train started and moved down the slope

Chapter Thirty Five

Since Nimal who comes home on other days at one o' clock didn't come home even at two o' clock. Maha Kumarihami and the others got worried " I'll give him today " threatened Maha Kumarihami.

Maha Kumarihami called Cecelia and asked her to go to the kachcheri and inform Mudiyanse Hamuduruwo that Nimal had not come home yet.

Cecelia went there and stood near the Mudliyar's room. The Mudliyar did not come there. Mr. Ariyadasa who saw her standing there inquired from her why she had come. Mr. Ariyadasa told Cecelia that the Mudliyar has been in the Government Agent's room from morning and that it's doubtful whether he will come out of it till evening.

Cecelia came to the bungalow and informed her of this. The Kumarihami who heard this started thinking.

That day Nelum Bandara came late even for his afternoon meal. He was in a troubled state of mind. What he ate was also very little. The wife asked him about it. Yet he did not give a correct reply. He went back also in great haste. Kumarihami's thoughts about these too were varied.

Three o' clock passed-Nimal did not come still. Four o' clock struck but Nimal still did not come.

" That fellow might have run away today too " said Maha Kumarihami in anger.

Four thirty too passed

" Where? He too is not come " said Kumarihami in anger; grumbling and looking at the kachcheri.

Just then Ariyadasa came there. He greeted her and stepped in to the bungalow.

" Sit down " said Kumarihami making an effort to hide her troubled mind.

" Not necessary "

" Mudalithuma said that there is some work and as it is getting late to take a hiring car and bring the children " said Ariyadasa.

" Why, is there any trouble? " asked Maha Kumarihami.

" I don't know " said Ariyadasa and as if Ariyadasa was going for some urgent work he greeted her and went back in a hurry. Cecelia went to bring James's hiring car. It's a white numbered car which is given on hire. In the meantime Maha Kumarihami and the daughter - in - law dressed up.

" Look will you this boy too is not here today ". said Maha Kumarihami in anger.

They went to Hemantha Vidyalaya and after taking Maithri they went to Vasantha Vidyalaya. Children were playing in the grounds Sunil knows quite well James's car.

Before this too the Kumarihami and others took this car and brought the children back from school. Immediately after the car is parked Sunil comes running. That day he did not come

" Go and look James "

James went and questioned the boys

" Don't know... Don't know...Don't know... " said all of them. One boy said " In the afternoon he did not even come to the class " and went off to play

James told this to Kumarihami.

They got worried, where could Sunil be?

The two Kumarihamis went in search of the school principal. He was in the office. He got up and respectfully received them. They informed the principal why they had come in very excited voices. The principal looked into the matter. It was found that Sunil was in his class in the morning, ate his food just as on other days and that he had not come to class in the afternoon. His book bag was also found in the class.

" The boy who brings the food too did not come home still" said the Maha Kumarihami.

The two women started crying. Kumarihami started crying as well as sobbing. In order to pacify them the principal told them all sorts of things. " We will look for them. Sometimes we don't know whether they went to the cinema. Don't know whether they had come home by now "said the principal.

" All this is because of that wild boy " said the Maha Kumarihami. Maithri too shed tears. The two women and Maithri got into the car and went back as quickly as possible.

" Cecelia did Appo come? " asked Kumarihami and rushed into the house.

" No "

" Nima? "

" He also hasn't "

" Mudiyanse Hamuduruwo "

" Has not come yet "

Kumarihami like a mad woman went towards the kachcheri. Maha Kumarihami too followed her. Still the Government Agent's office was open. The peon came running towards her

" Can we meet the Mudiyanse Hamuduruwo? "

" I don't know. Today there is a big inquiry "

" What is it? "

" Against Mudiyanse Hamuduruwo "

" What for? " asked the Kumarihami standing on her toes and peeping over the screen.

The Government Agent, the Assistant Government Agent, a Police officer, several others and Nelum Bandara were there The clock showed five thirty.

" What is the inquiry? " asked the Maha Kumarihami from the peon.

" A bribery complaint Ayubowan; who knows whether they are true or false? " said the peon with the desire of consoling her. The Kumarihami too heard the words of the peon.

" Please excuse me ", said the Kumarihami and went in to the office. All stood up. She looked at the husband and said "Putha is not there ", and collapsed. The Police officer rushed forward and held her and stopped her from falling

Chapter Thirty Six

At five thirty the Colombo train left Polgahawela. Somebody came and sat beside Nimal. What? Sunil?

" Sunil " he said in a low voice

Nimal could not believe his eyes

" Why is this Sunil? "

The two friends got up and straining their necks out of the compartment and without being heard by the passengers opened their conversation.

Sunil explained how he came to the Railway station after he ate the afternoon meal and how he came out of school and boarded the bus to get to the station. He also explained how he barely got into the train when it was whistling, how at Peradeniya he looked for him and at Kadugannawa saw him drinking tea He further explained how he could not get into the correct compartment.

" Money for the train? "

" I too brought my money till "

"Why? "

" To buy what you said you were buying "

Sunil showed his purse which contained eighteen rupees and some cents.

Nimal in a way was happy. Again to converse with Sunil, to be with him, to go on journeys he was very pleased. But how is Sunil going to school, what is Sunil going to do Nimal can do some work at some household. But Sunil ?

On the other hand Sunil suffers all these because of Nimal isn't it? When the parents hear about Sunil running away what will happen? About Nimal of course the police will be informed and a postcard will be sent to his father and that will be the end. But to find Sunil how much would they tire themselves. Since Sunil is running away Nimal too might get caught.

Nimal was wearing a white shirt and a red sarong. Sunil a white shirt and a pair of blue shorts, a grey pair of socks and black shoes. Their difference was clearly seen by their dress. Their appearances and looks could easily pass of as almost belonging to the same class. Sunil slowly pulled out his shoes and socks. After a little while he took them out and without being seen by anybody threw them out. Nimal who saw this silently watched him in wonder.

At Alauwa a Tamil boy and girl climbed into the compartment with two drums with bells tied to them. They were smaller than Sunil.

" Ha there comes the musicians " said a traveller.

After the train started the two children sang a Hindi song to the music of the drums. They sang it beautifully. While singing they held their palms to the travellers. The travellers too gave them one, two or sometimes five cents. The two friends too gave them two cents each. They remembered their Gemunu school play.

" If we too have two drums like that we could sing Virindu and find money isn't it? " asked Nimal

Buddha Dhamma Sangha we worship the Triple Gem
We'll sing a little Virindu about our great Land
That's very good; that's very good,
Kings Gemunu and Perakumba who adorned our Sri Lanka,
Never bowed their heads to aliens but always held them erect
That's quite true; that's quite true,
To go with great honour past the grave of an enemy king
Who else but a Sinhala King would make such abiding laws
That's quite true; That's quite true,
To the beggar who was fed by him he gave his noble head
Where else does a Siri Sangabo King live except in Sri
Lanka
That's also true; that's also true
Before his execution like a lion cub he cried
Noble son Madduma Bandara; in what country does he live!
Where else but in Sri Lanka
The hoisted flag was put down to save our country's honour
Bow your heads dear friends to our Wariyapola young priest
Sadu, sadu, sadu, sadu
If I 've made any errors to desecrate your name
Pardon me mother Lanka I worship you with both my hands.
Please, I too worship
Sunil began crying, " Mother, Mother "
" Why Sunil? " Nimal asked seeing this.
" Mother and others will be looking for us, isn't it? "
" Sunil you get back then by the next train " said Nimal.
" My mother came to my mind and I cried. I have no
desire to go home " said Sunil.
" But anyway, I like very much if Sunil goes back "
At Ragama a big crowd of people got in. The travellers were

huddled up. Some of them were standing. After they passed Kelaniya Sunil asked Nimal, " Is it very much further away? ". Nimal said by heart the list of Railway stations in his Geography book. " Colombo Fort, Maradana, Kelaniya, Hunupitiya " then he stopped and continued "After this Maradana and then Fort " he said.

" Are you getting down at Fort? " asked Sunil.

" I bought the ticket to Fort " said Nimal and taking the ticket he examined it. Sunil too, put his hand into his pocket and exclaimed." My purse isn't there ", and in his excitement put his hand in his trouser pockets and shirt pocket and looked for it. The two friends in excitement got up from their seats and looked on the tops of their seats, under the seats and everywhere.

" My ticket was in it " said Sunil looking frightened.

" What are you looking for ", asked a gentleman.

" My purse is not there " said Sunil crying.

". Where did you lose it? " asked the gentleman.

" At Polgahawela it was there " said Nimal.

" Look, look " said the gentleman.

They all looked for it everywhere. The gentleman too looked for it with interest. He was middle aged and very fat. He wore a coat and a pair of trousers. He looked distinguished.

" From where are you both coming? " asked the gentleman.

" From Kandy " said Sunil.

" Did you both come together? "

" No, yes " said Sunil

" Why no, yes, two? " asked the gentleman in a high tone.

" Where are you going? '

" Colombo " said Sunil

" What part of Colombo? "

The boys looked at each others faces. The gentleman seeing this questioned the two boys separately. Since none of the boys could give a reply to the question, a few travellers laughed.

" Tissa Vidyalaya " uttered Sunil.

" What for? " the gentleman went on questioning

Both were silent.

" These two are running away somewhere " someone said.

" Yes, yes " said a few in support.

The two boys in fear looked here and there They looked at each other and breathed hard.

" You are ruining away isn't it? " asked the gentleman in a hoarse voice and a fearful face.

The two boys started to cry together The travellers laughed Just at that moment the train stopped at the Fort Railway station The clock showed seven thirty.

" Come here " said the man and holding them by their hands they alighted from the train and walked along the platform

Chapter Thirty Seven

That evening itself the Kandy Police inquired into the disappearance of Sunil and Nimal. Maha Kumarihami had informed the Police that Nimal had taken fifty rupees away.

" How do you know whether it was taken away by Sunil or Nimal " asked the Police officer.

" Our children never do such things. And the other thing is that I saw the boy Nima loitering in the room in the afternoon. I did not take an interest in it at that time " said Maha Kumarihami as if displeased.

" That is correct. I just asked about it: don't get angry " said the Policeman kindly, becoming aware that she had lost her temper.

Kumarihami was kissing an old shirt of Sunil and sobbing and crying. It was not easy to console Maithri. When she sees the mother crying she cries more and more.

" Cecelia see whether the car is coming " said Kumarihami from time to time through her tears.

" Not yet " said Cecelia.

At eight in the evening the car arrived. Kumarihami ran to the verandah. Nelum Bandara alighted from the car.

" Was he there? " both asked together. Both did not get answers.

Kumarihami crying very loud tumbled into the chair. Maha Kumarihami tied a ' Pandura ' for the second time. Nelum Bandara had come after going to Nelumpura in order to meet

Muthu Banda.

Muthu Banda had informed him that Nimal had not come there and that he will inform Nelum Bandara, even by a telegram, if he gets any kind of information.

That night no one at Maya bungalow ate dinner. All slept wherever they liked. Nelum Bandara remained in his office room smoking cigarettes. Kumarihami wearing what she wore in the afternoon reclined in the sofa in different ways from time to time. Maha Kumarihami drank coffee and went here and there. The clock struck twelve. Maha Kumarihami went towards the office room. Nelum Bandara was still there smoking cigarettes and thinking.

" How is the inquiry into the petition, son " she asked.

" Let our problem be over " said Nelum Bandara getting up in anger and going towards the bathroom.

" When things happens one follows another. All these are as a reason of that wretch....... " she said biting her teeth.

As one o' clock struck someone knocked at the door.

" Who is it? " Nelum Bandara asked and got up.

" From the Police " was the answer.

Nelum Bandara opened the door. All rushed into the verandah.

" The two boys are there " said the Police officer smiling.

The mother sprawled on the floor and cried.

" Where? " asked the father.

" Colombo "

The Maha Kumarihami raised the hands and worshipped the Maligawa. Cecelia ran and put Maithri up and broke the news.

She too came out. Palingumenika too kept her hand on her chest.

" Tomorrow the two boys will be brought before the court. Then the boys can be taken over " explained the Police officer.

" Our chief asked me now itself to inform you; that is why I came during the night itself. Are you going to Colombo tomorrow? "

" Yes we are going now itself " said the mother snivelling.

" That's all right. I 'll see you later " said the Policeman. He smiled and wishing them got on to the bike and rode off.

Chapter Thirty Eight

Sunil and Nimal were produced before the Colombo Magistrate's court. The charge brought against Sunil was that he travelled in the train without a ticket. The lawyer's explanation of the background to the strange incident was believed by the court which accepted the money paid by the father of the accused. Sunil who belonged to a respectable family promised that he would never again run away from home; and on that promise he was handed over to his father.

The charge against Nimal was more serious than that: it was the theft of fifty rupees.

The court asked whether anybody was appearing for Nimal. There was no answer. The next question was whether any custodian or any relative had come to court. Sunil looked humbly at his father; he was silent. It was brought to light that the accused's father had been given notice about this case through the Nelumpura Police. Yet the court ordered that he was to be kept under the custody of Fiscal till next Friday.

The Fiscal's officer took Nimal away from court. Nelum Bandara left court with Sunil.

Sunil looked back and saw Nimal going with the Fiscal's officer. He looked at Sunil with a look of fear mixed with a mild smile.

Kumarihami did not come to court. She was in the car itself seated. She saw the father and Sunil coming towards her. She covered her eyes with the fall of the sari. Sunil came in fear and climbed into the rear seat of the car. Immediately the mother put her hands around Sunil's neck and keeping her face on his cried secretly. Sunil too quietly cried and sobbed.

The car left the place. No one spoke anything. The car stopped in front of the closest hotel. Nelum Bandara called a waiter and ordered him to bring a dozen mutton rolls to the car. The parents know that it's a thing that Sunil likes very much. The waiter brought the parcel and gave it. Nelum Bandara paid the bill and drove the car. While going in the car they ate the rolls. Sunil was reluctant to eat. Appachchi and mother ignored him and ate.

"Eat son " said the mother once again. After that he took a roll and ate. On other days he would eat three or four rolls. That day he only ate one. The mother and the father ate three rolls each and once again the car was stopped in front of another hotel.

" Two teas and one ice cream " said appachchi.

" Here son " said the mother giving the ice cream to Sunil.

He took it slowly. Appachchi and mother drank tea. Sunil that day took only two mouthfuls of ice cream. Nelum Bandara bought a slab of chocolate and gave it to the wife and drove the car along. Appachchi and mother did not speak at all. That was almost more than what Sunil could bear up. He thought that anger they had towards him had not subsided. If it is not that, he suspected that they would have quarrelled. Appachchi and amma quarrel very rarely. If they quarrel even they would not remain long without talking. Even Sunil could not understand the silence.

" What would happen to Nima kolla? " asked mother at the end.

" Let lightning strike him " said appachchi aloud. His tone was rough strong and fierce. He said this staring at her as if he were angry with mother.

" Everything happens to people isn't it; why are you then thinking so much " asked mother very kindly from appachchi.

"Please I 'll worship you, we'll go without talking " he said and drove the car at high speed.

The mother took the fall of her sari and wiped her tears. Sunil saw this and again he started shedding tears. He then cried aloud.

" What is it? " asked Nelum Bandara and stopped the car at a place where there were no houses.

" Please appachchi, don't get angry with me. Here I worship you " said Sunil.

" I didn't say that to you " said appachchi stroking his head with his left hand. " You don't worry son it's not for you " he said again and patted his back. Sunil encouraged by this said while crying, " Please appachchi don't get angry with Nimal also. I ran away alone while Nimal said ' don't ' "

" It's not that, it's another matter " said appachchi attempting to smile. The mother too cried again.

" Don't get angry with mother, appachchi " said Sunil still crying.

" I am not angry with mother, son " said appachchi looking at mother and then said " It's something different "

The mother too dried her tears and looking at the son she said " We are not angry son ". Yet she cried again.

Sunil did not understand anything.

Beside Sunil even Nelum Kumarihami was not aware of anything about the inquiry against the husband. He did not tell them anything. When they were going to Colombo and whenever she questioned him at any time about it he had asked her very strongly not to question him. Finally the mother started talking with the son.

" Where did you stay last night? "

Sunil answered softly,

" The Police Station "

" What did you eat? "

" Rice "

" Who handed you to the Police? "

" The Station Master "

Nelum Kumarihami did not question him further. She thought that her husband's pain of mind would increase. When she thought of her son's disobedience she felt the pain in her mind was almost unbearable.

Chapter Thirty Nine

As soon as the car was parked in front of ' Maya ' bungalow
Sunil went with his eyes downcast straight to his bed and slept.
Muthu Banda stood in the courtyard and worshipped Nelum
Bandara and Kumarihami.

" Why didn't you go to Colombo? " asked Nelum
Bandara.

" The Police of course came last night and told me.
They said that you too were also informed; therefore I did not
send a telegram " narrated Muthu Banda.

" It's not that man; why didn't you come to Colombo? "
asked Nelum Bandara again.

" Even my dog will not go in search of him "

" Now, the case is on Friday next, if you want to take
custody of the boy go and see " said Nelum Bandara.

" Even if they tell me that lightning has struck him this
father is not the one who will go. If he had smeared ash on your
golden faces there is nothing for me to do. I am not going.... I
am not going.... I am not going " he said in order to convince
himself.

" Did you eat anything? " asked Kumarihami.

" Yes, I ate. I waited so long only to see Sudu Appo. I
am going home now. May I take leave of you " he said and
worshipped her and with pain of mind stepped on to the road

Muthu Banda left with a heavy heart. To attend to those matters he neither had money nor the time. If he saves Nimal and comes home he may lose the hut where they live. Therefore Muthu Banda talking only of the bad side of his son and reminding himself of it made up his mind. He even told his wife the same.

Chapter Forty

Before a quarter of an hour passed after Nelum Bandara came home the Government Agent's peon came. Maha Kumarihami who saw his coming said, " Now that man came twice and asked whether son is in "

" Why? " Nelum Bandara asked the peon.

" Aibowan, the Government Agent asked you to come for a moment "

" Why, is there some trouble? "

" Don't know Aibowan "

Nelum Bandara was shocked. He went towards the bath room.

" What is it? " Kumarihami asked the peon.

" The Government Agent asked Mudiyanse Hamuduruwo to come "

" Why, is there any trouble? " asked the Kumarihami.

" Don't know Aibowan; was Podi Appo brought? "

" Yes " said Kumarihami.

" May I go? " said the peon and he went away.

" I shall go and come back " said Nelum Bandara and stepped on to the courtyard.

Exactly at this time the firewood woman came directly in front of him.

" Son remain a little and proceed " said Maha Kumarihami drawing a breath.

Nelum Bandara listened to his mother and waited for a little while before proceeding towards the kachcheri. The Government Agent was waiting for him.

" Please sit down ". Nelum Bandara sat down.

" Did you bring the boy? "

" Yes "

" I am very happy about it " said the Government Agent, and continued " Nelum Bandara, what we call troubles come to people one after another. That is natural. No one could stop that. Another thing is that when we do our duty, in very many instances we have to do very pleasant things as well as very unpleasant things ".

Nelum Bandara listened to his talk restlessly.

" What I have got to do today is a very sad duty ". The Government Agent saying this brought a typed letter from the table and gave one copy to him. Saying " sign this stating that you have accepted this letter " he showed the other copy also to him.

Nelum Bandara's eyes suffered a black out and he felt as if his head was turning. He also felt as if he didn't hear. He signed the copy and taking the letter looked at it. It was stated there that as a reason of a bribery charge his work has been suspended from that day. He was covered with a cold sweat.

" I pray that you will be released from this charge " the Government Agent said and shook hands with him.

Nelum Bandara with great effort smiled a little and said respectfully, " Thank you very much ".

He put the letter in his pocket and after coming out of the room he put on a happy face somehow and waving his hand to the onlookers and greeting them he walked down the steps and came away.

Chapter Forty One

Until Nelum Bandara went home the mother and the wife waited in the verandah impatiently. Yet no one spoke to him When Nelum Bandara was hurt they knew that he does not like anyone talking to him. The mother and the wife were looking at him.

" He just asked me to come about some matter " he said and went into his room. The Kumarihamis too went thought-fully to attend to their work separately.

If the charges are to be proved how will he get caught he thought. The secret about the money obtained to certify the vouchers would be exposed only if Ariyadasa and the colonists go against him. Ariyadasa would not do such a thing. It is because if he does it he would also get caught. The farmers too would not do such a callous thing. It's because they thought that the ' Unnanse ' of the kachcheri had helped them always.

The most fearful charges would not be that. One would be the payments that the colonists who did not do anything received. The other would be the receipt of money by forgery. Nelum Bandara again began smoking cigarettes. He walked about the room. He started talking to himself. He shook his shoulders. He raised both his arms up. Shook his head. He walked one or two feet and stopped.

Nelum Kumarihami heard him talking alone. She opened the door a little and peeped. She saw his funny actions and with deep sorrow she closed the door and went back. She went and sat near the dining table and kept her face on her hands.

Maha Kumarihami also saw how her daughter - in - law was and in anger looked at her and cast a sigh. She went towards the door and stood there and thought for a while. She heard the son talking to himself and also the sound of his footfalls. She then went towards her daughter-in-law quickly.

" Daughter " she called aloud. The daughter-in-law looked at her startled. Maha Kumarihami called her.

" There must be an end to this. Come here to ask what this is" she said and holding the daughter-in-law's hand she went towards the son's room and tapped at the door and called in anger " Son, son"

" What is it " asked Nelum Bandara in a harsh voice.

Maha Kumarihami opened the door and entered the room together with the daughter-in-law.

" Tell me what your trouble is " she asked in a forceful voice.

" No one need know them " answered the son.

" Not anyone; this is your wife and I am your mother "

" So "

" So we want to know what it is "

" We cannot remain like ' Billo ' , can we! " said the wife without any fear.

" The other thing is that if there is some trouble can you solve it by smoking cigarettes. You must do what there is to be done" said the mother also.

" By telling these it is of no use " said the son.

" How do you know? " asked the mother.

" Then shall I tell you? " he asked staring and biting his teeth.

" That is what we are asking you " said the mother frowning and frightened.

" I am interdicted " he said raising his voice and added "There I said it "

" Can you remain silent without telling it; what is it after all?" asked the mother suppressing her sorrow and her fear.

" Worse things happen to people " said the wife forcing a smile.

Nelum Bandara who heard these words thought of embracing the mother as well as the wife together. How have they cultivated the power of tolerance so much? What he expected was for the mother and the wife to cry and weep having thrown themselves on the ground. He even thought that the mother would even get a heart attack. Helpless Nelum Bandara does not know the minds of his mother and wife. He did not know that his mother even wished the earth would open up to hide herself. He also did not know that his wife felt as if she received a blow on her head from a club and her whole body was benumbed. He also did not know that the mother and daughter acted like two great actresses at that moment. By their words he was encouraged.

" All this is the work of Kandalande ." he said.

From this a new strength was born to the Maha Kumarihami. As a reason of the son's fault she felt that half of the burden fell on her.

" Why is that? " asked his wife.

" He is the one who now works on the colonies. He goes through the old papers and gets people, one by one, to rake up the past irregularities " said the husband.

" Why? What he took from the renters? " the mother asked angrily.

" That is a different matter " said the son.

" Then it is those people who live in glass houses that throw stones? " said the mother staring at the ' Ruhunu ' bungalow.

"Come, come eat a little rice. After I found my boy I don't mind any other things happening to us " said the wife who went holding her husband's hand.

" Then what else? Are we to die for these things " said the mother too following.

Nelum Bandara never realized the value of his mother and his wife more than on that day. Since the children had eaten dinner and slept the three elders ate their dinner happily as if they had acquired a new life.

Chapter Forty Two

The pain in their minds of course did not diminish. The three of them thought about the future alone. Maha Kumarihami was thinking how to ignore Kandalanda and lay sprawled on her bed. Kumarihami was in Maithri's room not to be seen by the husband, not to be noticed by him and not to be felt by him. She cried embracing the pillow.

From that day the husband was to receive only half his salary. With this how could he attend to his affairs? She did not know that her husband earned money illegally. It was true that he went for the races to Colombo on Saturdays. Similarly almost every day he went to his club. She was aware that at the club he drank a little. The Maha Kumarihami too was aware of this. That was because people of some social standing both in Kandy and Nelumpura did these. Kandalande too went to Colombo on Saturdays without fail. At the beginning both went together. After their rift they went separately.

Nelum Bandara did not have more than seven hundred rupees in his Bank. Kumarihami too did not have more than seven hundred and fifty rupees in the Post Office Savings Bank. In regard to property what they had were the land of Aluth Walauwa and the Galwale land. The Galwale land was written in favour of Maha Kumarihami. It was with the dowry given to Nelum Kumarihami that the car was purchased as well as a part of the purchase price of Galwale land. Thinking of all sorts of matters like these and suffering great pain of mind the wife lay on the bed.

She got up from bed as if she had sensed some thing and went to the husband's room. He was seated at the table and writing some thing.

" What is this? " she asked and immediately afterwards like a person who had seen a ghost or like one who had gone insane the husband jumped from his seat, and saying " Go, go, go "pushed his wife. Her body stuck the door and the door closed.

He had staring eyes . His hair was dishevelled. " What's this?" the wife shouted in fear, suspicion and in anger. The husband rushed at her. He held her throat in his right hand and opened the door with his left and attempted to push her out. At the same time Maha Kumarihami saying " What's this? " rushed into the room and attempted to separate the two. But without releasing the wife he stretched his left hand towards the mother. Just as when a snake bites a person he in a moment released both his hands and as if he were trying break his own fingers caught hold of his hands and stared. In a moment he fell on his stomach on the bed and wept like a child.

The mother went up to him and kept her hand on his forehead; the head was very warm. She went in to the adjoining room and brought Eau-de-cologne and put it gently on his head. He then closed his eyes. The wife brought the blanket and covered him. In a short while he started groaning.

The mother nodded her head and by a sign asked " What happened? " The daughter-in-law too by a sign answered " do not know " and she went up to the table and took a letter that was being written by her husband and read it silently. The mother too came there and looked at the letter.

" Drunkenness, Racing and Bribery are responsible for my death. The taking away of my life is for the others...... " it was at this time that the wife had entered the room. The mother and the wife were very frightened. The wife opened the drawer. The pistol was there. The wife removed it and hid it in the room further away, and returned shedding tears.

"I thought by now you had hidden it " said the mother as she gave a long sigh. She kept a chair near the son's bed and sat down. She took the " Buddha Adahilla " and read it silently. The wife sat in a place not visible to the husband, and observed him carefully.

As there were only about three hours for daybreak they did not want to summon the doctor.

Nelum Bandara slept till eleven o'clock in the morning. The moment he awoke he ran up to the table and examined it. He opened the drawer and looked inside. He then went back and sprawled on the bed again. The wife who saw that the husband was awake sent a glass of water and a cup of tea to him through Maithri.

" Appachchi, here's tea " she said.

Appachchi rinsed his mouth, sat on his bed, held the cup of tea brought by the daughter and holding her against his chest kissed her.

" Daughter, didn't you go to school today? "

" No "

" Why? "

" It's Saturday, isn't it? "

" Right, right. Where's brother? "

" He is there, in fear of appachchi "

" Sunil " appachchi called the son.

" Appachchi "

" Come here "

Sunil came slowly; frightened.

" The fellow is here in fear " said the wife coming there with a smile.

Sunil who heard it cried aloud.

" Come here, you rogue " said appachchi and making him sit on his lap said " Those things that are gone are gone son; now don't anybody say about them in this house " he said and kissed his head.

" Brother is in fear of what the schoolboys would say" said Maithri.

" I will explain it to the school authorities and have it stopped. Now go and play " said appachchi.

" Water has been kept for you to wash your face " said the wife to the husband with a kind and smiling face.

The husband did not still look at the wife. He raised his head. Their eyes met. The wife still showing her smile and biting her small finger looked aside.

" Then why did you embrace the pillow and cry? " asked the husband.

" When? "

" At dead of night "

She came to know that her husband had seen her crying secretly.

" So when I cry, what's there? " she asked.

" As a reason of that only all these things happened ' he said and covered his face with both his hands.

" I never thought that you are so foolish " said the wife and sat close to him.

Chapter Forty Three

In a ' Malpala ' made of gokkola half a papaw into which oil had been poured had been lit by Muthu Banda and Ranmenika, who besought the Gods for one full week and handed over Nimal to their care at the end.

They came to know from newspapers that Mudliyar Nelum Bandara's work had been suspended. " If such things happen to high ups why should we repent? May the Gods look after us, that is all we have to say " said Muthu Banda. Continuously from Friday Muthu Banda met a Police officer from Nelumpura whom he knew and inquired about his son from him. But no news about Nimal was published. On the fourth day he received news about Nimal from this Police officer. It was that he had been sent to a Juvenile reformatory for one year.

" It's good there friend; either the boy will grow up well or turn out to be extremely bad; but that boy will not be bad " concluded the Policeman.

" What else can I do Ralahamy? To us it's only the help of the Gods " said Muthu Banda and thanking him profusely he went away.

When Ranmenika heard the news she started crying.

" I swear by my mother, what has happened to you. Ralahamy also told this either the boy will be good or extremely bad. It's either merit or sin; that's all. Whatever happens he will get rice for the two meals; it's not like this " said Muthu Banda and consoled his wife.

Sunil of course remembered Nimal often. On Friday he remembered Nimal very clearly. But Sunil does not speak about Nimal to anyone now. Through fear he's silent.

Sunil goes to Vasantha Vidyalaya again. At the beginning the children played the fool of him by calling him ' Kale Sunil '. But after the teacher punished them that name gradually died away. But some secretly without being heard by Sunil used the name.

As a reason of his own troubles Nelum Bandara too forgot Nimal. One day he accidentally met the Police officer who inquired into the escapade of the two boys. He came to know from him what happened to Nimal. Nelum Bandara informed his wife as well as the mother about this. Once when Sunil was arguing with his sister Maithri the mother intervened and scolded Sunil.

" Do you know what happened to your friend? "

" What friend? "

" To Nimal "

The name itself made Sunil silent.

" He went to prison for one year. If you too were allowed to go it would have been fine " she said.

Sunil was put into great pain of mind. He thought it was because of him that Nimal fell into trouble. But he did not mention anything about it. He often thought about Nimal's prison life and cried. What is going into prison? Is it being asked to remain without food? Is it to be put inside a dark room with door closed? Is it being tied tightly and left alone?

Sunil was frightened to question about it from anyone either at school or at home.

After two weeks of the case Muthu Banda received a letter from Nimal. Amitha read it out so that it could be heard by anyone.

My dear Appachchi,

I am well. I did not come home that day thinking that appachchi and the others would be driven away from the quarry. For all the wrongs I did excuse me. I will study again, not only books but carpentry also. When I come home after one year I will be able to help appachchi more. Then if it is not good for me to come there I shall work at some other place and shall send money to appachchi. By the help of the Gods I hope my mother is quite well. Is chuti Nangi now big? Will she be able to recognize me? Remembering mother, elder sister brothers younger sisters I shall stop.

Your loving son,
Nimal.

As Amitha read the letter she paused several times. She wiped her tears. Ranmenika too sobbed loudly several times. After the letter was read Muthu Banda with tear filled eyes laughed loudly, saying, that's merit and sin.

Little sister and the brothers clapped their hands rhythmically saying, " A letter from brother ", " A letter from brother. " That evening itself Muthu Banda wrote a letter in reply Ranmenika was breast feeding the little daughter seated beside Muthu Banda. She is now very much better. Amitha wrote the letter just as her father asked her.

Galwale Gedara.
Nelumgama.
Nelumpura.

May the triple gem help you,

My dear putha,

The reason why I am writing this is to inform you that I received your letter. We are very happy because of it. To hear that you are living there happily pleases us. Wherever you are stay happily that is what is needed. Everything happens according to our merit and sins. Nobody can stop those. That is how it is in our religion. Be good with the gentlemen who are there. Learn your work well. Say the precepts morning and evening. Bestow merit on the Gods. In your name we lit a 'Malpala ' for a week. Now we light pahan on Wednesday and Saturdays. We are getting on well. To you and to those who are there we wish you the blessings of the Triple Gem.

Your Loving farther,
G. G. Muthu Banda.

Chapter Forty Four

Three months passed after Nelum Bandara was interdicted. No action whatsoever had been taken in respect of his service in the Government. He had realized that instead of facing problems it's foolish to play hide and seek with them. He had also realized that without trying to free yourself from some sorrow if you attempt to run away from it you will have to face more and more new sorrows. This he had realized well.

If he had committed suicide that day what would have been the fate of the two children, the wife and the fate of the mother, the disgrace they had to face, and how much the pain of mind would it have been he thought.

As a reason of the bribery charges the sorrow and the distress that they would be subject to would be hundredfold if he had committed suicide. This he had now understood clearly. By committing suicide he could put an end to his problem in this world. But who can say what would happen in the next world. How can one say what the extent of shame would be to his future generation. Will not the future generation curse his grave. Nelum Bandara began thinking about all sorts of things.

Nelum Bandara now spends a new life. He does not drink; does not back horses and does not go to clubs.

He sold his car. The children go to school by bus. They take bread in the morning and eat it in the afternoon. The Kumarihamis too do their work themselves. Cecelia went home.

As Palingumenika has no place to go she does the household work with pleasure even without a salary. The children too do their work themselves.

Sunil likes this new life very much. He is secretly happy as he is getting used to it like Nimal.

Maha Kumarihami did all sorts of things in order to save her son. She met all the powerful people that she knew and pleaded with them to save him. Some said that they could not interfere in such matters straightaway. Some said that they will make an effort to do so. Some promised that somehow they will save him. She had to spend large sums of money by way of expenses in order to attend to these matters. She had to mortgage the Galwale property for seven thousand rupees. There were no obstacles for this from the son or the daughter-in-law.

Nelum Bandara has no friends now. It is very seldom that a car stops at Maya bungalow now. It is also rarely that an important person stops a car there. Sometimes only a farmer brings some vegetables and goes away keeping them.

After the lapse of a further three months the charges framed against Nelum Bandara were presented to court. Maha Kumarihami who heard it lost her self-restraint.

" Everything what I did turned out to be as if I had cut stakes and cast them into the river ". She hit her head. She hit her chest. " I will tell them everything and come " said Maha Kumarihami walking to and fro.

" Don't make them angry, mother; we might even be able to get their help for the case " said the daughter in law.

Now Nelum Bandara believes in fate also. He does not get angry suddenly. He's not unnecessarily hasty. He does not become happy, nor does he become sad. A well-known Astrologer had told him that he would have a bad time in the future. Therefore he does what should be done without any neglect on his part and he leaves matters to fate and remains silent.

After the case was filed it was not necessary to remain in Kandy spending a huge sum of money thought Nelum Bandara.

" Mother, now it is useless staying here; we will go home" said Nelum Bandara to Maha Kumarihami.

" Why? "

" Why do we stay here spending a large sum of money. Is there any use? "

" Do you say that you'll lose the case? "

" I don't say that. If I win I'll come back. If I lose I'll remain in the village "

" Isn't it better to remain here if you win; if you lose go to the village " argued the Maha Kumarihami.

" It is better to get used to it earlier " said the son.

Maha Kumarihami disagreed with the son's proposal, but the wife accepted what the husband said.

After Nelum Bandara went to the village and informed the D.R.O of his views and problems, he promised to vacate Aluth Walauwa and give him vacant possession of the house by the end of the month. Nelum Bandara profusely thanked him. When the Maha Kumarihami heard the news she was happy to go back to the village.

The Nelum family again went back to the Aluth Walauwa to reside. When they came from Kandy even Ariyadasa was not there to wish them. That was because he feared that he would be drawn into the case. Only the caretaker of the bungalow was there to receive the key.

Sunil came to the village very happily. Since the children of Vasantha Vidyalaya called him often ' Kale Sunil ' stealthily he was very happy to leave the school and come. Maithri of course liked Kandy better than the village.

Again Maithri was admitted to Nelumpura Vihara Maha Devi Vidyalaya and Sunil to Gemunu Vidyalaya. They went to school and came back on foot. Sunil went to school very happily and returned from school very happily. Maithri often grumbled about it.

" Wait Duwa, until a good time comes to buy a car " said aththamma.

Chapter Forty Five

Nelum Bandara's case was heard in court. A lengthy account of it appeared in the newspapers daily. The case went on for five days.

Young Nimal too read the news about the case with a great interest. As all the main papers were available at the reading room of the Reformatory it was easy for him to read. No sooner the afternoon meal is over he runs there and goes through all the papers. Everyday photographs about the case too appeared. On the first day it was a photograph of Nelum Bandara talking to his lawyers.

" The lawyers of course are the best available " Nimal heard what was being spoken by the chief of the Reformatory to his assistant.

Nimal did not understand everything that was published. But as a reason of the case he came to know a great deal that was said about it.

One day there was a photograph of the witnesses. He easily recognized Ariyadasa in it. Similarly there were several photographs of farmers who had visited ' Maya ' bungalow .

On the third day Kandalanda's photograph was published. Certain documents which were in his care at the kachcheri were produced by him. He mentioned that he saw colonists with all kinds of gifts coming to ' Maya ' bungalow. Nimal thought that the answers given by Kandalanda to questions put to him at the cross examination revealed that he too was also one who accepted bribes.

As a reason of the petition sent against Kandalanada to the Government Agent regarding bribery the fact that Kandalanda was not given the post of Mudliyar was revealed. He accepted that tax collectors visited ' Ruhunu ' bungalow when he stayed there and that Kandalanda family and Nelum family were not on good terms for a long time.

On the fifth day Nelum Bandara had given evidence. Those proceedings were very long. Most of the record contained what Nimal did not understand. From what he understood Nimal felt deeply sad. Thinking that his friends would see his sad face he raised the paper to cover his face and read the newspaper.

The Nelum family now stays at Nelumgama. They went there about five months back. At first they stayed at the Aluth Walauwa. Now they stay in a temporary coconut thatch covered house. Moratu Mudalali now stays at the Aluth Walauwa. The Walauwa property and the Galwale property was mortgaged for fifteen thousand rupees to the bank. The Galwale property was mortgaged first. The Walauwa property was mortgaged for the purpose of the expenses of the case. Nelum Bandara now has only rupees seventy five. In Kumarihami's pass book there is only Five hundred rupees. Apart from the furniture and jewellery worth about one thousand rupees they do not have anything by way of wealth.

Maithri and Sunil were removed from the Kandy schools since they could not bear up the expenses. When Nimal became aware of this he cried. He remembered the day when he had to leave school because his father was not able to bear up the expenses He prayed that Sunil be spared from such a thing. The reason was because Sunil did not know to break stones, or drive buffaloes or to work with a mammoty.

Since news about the Nelum family were not mentioned in appachchi's letters Nimal was wondering why it was and he was greatly worried.

Chapter Forty Six

The following day after the noon meal when Nimal as usual was running towards the reading room the big bell rang. The boys were distressed. That bell rings in order to get the boys to the hall. Nimal too together with the other boys ran into the hall. All the fifty eight resident boys were there. They questioned one another as to what the reason was. None was able to give the correct reply to this.

In a little while the principal and a middle aged lady came there. She was big built and her hair was curly. Her knot of hair was also big. There were gray hairs here and there. She was copper coloured. She wore a light blue blouse and a light blue sari. Her shoes were black.

As she entered the hall the boys stood up and wished her 'Ayubowan' and worshipped her. The lady too bowed her head and putting her hands together, smiled and greeted them. After the principal and the lady took their seats on the stage the boys too sat down.

The principal stood up and then addressed the boys. " Boys although you may not have seen this lady before she is a noble lady who has done immense service for your well-being. This honourable lady had donated vast sums of money for a few reformatories like this and for other meritorious work. She did not come here for some time as she had gone to many countries abroad. We have talked about her to you several times. She is the president of the Sri Lanka Samaja Sewa Sangamaya. We got you together at this time in order that she could see you " said the principal and sat down.

The president of the Samaja Sewa Sangamaya stood up. The principal and the boys greeted her by clapping their hands.

" Boys I came today for a very important matter. The principal has given you a short description of our Sri Lanka Samaja Sewa Sangamaya and me. Our Samaja Sewa Sangamaya gives to a Lama Niwasa a scholarship annually. It has been done for the past several years without a break. This year our Board of Directors have decided to award a scholarship to this reformatory." According to the gesture of the principal all present smiled and clapped their hands.

" That scholarship will be given to the best boy of the reformatory, to the best boy in morality, in handicrafts and in learning. We will set up a trust for the selected boy to study up to the highest class in a boarding school; therefore we have informed your principal several days earlier to select the best boy and present him today. I now invite the principal to introduce the selected student to us "

The president amidst the clapping sat down. The boys looked here and there. Each boy according to his thoughts directed his eyes towards the boy that he thought is the best.

The principal stood up amidst the clapping of hands for the president. The boys too followed her.

" Honourable Madam, boys, I must first thank the president of the Sri Lanka Samaja Sewa Sangamaya who is the lady who is with us here now for having selected our reformatory for the prize. " The boys clapped.

" To select the best boy is a difficult task. That responsibility I did not fully put on myself. It is on the advice of the officials of our reformatory who are in charge of all the branches; education, handicrafts, art and morality, that the best boy suitable for the scholarship was chosen. "

After this the principal, like an actor, was a little silent and looking here and there increased the anxiety of the boys.

The principal then said raising his voice, " The best boy in our reformatory is ' Galwalegedara Nimal ' "

Nimal was shocked and looked here and there as if he could not believe what he heard. All the eyes of the boys fell on him. Some of the boys said " We thought Nimal would be selected "

" Nimal stand up and greet us " ordered the principal.

Nimal stood up and putting his hands together worshipped her.

" Nimal come here " said the principal.

Nimal went up to the stage as if in a dream. The principal whispered into his ears and said something. Accordingly Nimal bowed put his hands together and greeted her. She asked Nimal about his family and stroked his head. She wished him and got up from her chair. The boys also accordingly got up and remained standing. The president again addressed the boys and said, " In order to win the scholarship next year from now onwards work resolutely. May you live long. " She concluded and set out to leave.

" May you live long " greeted the boys loudly.

Immediately after the principal and the lady left the boys went up to Nimal and in different words expressed their happiness. Nimal accepted their blessings and their praise modestly. Nimal's face appeared as if his mind was occupied by something far away.

Nimal as accustomed went straight to the reading room and looked for the page in the newspaper devoted to court cases. He saw a full photograph of Nelum Bandara. Underneath the photograph was the word ' Accused '. In one corner was the group photograph of the two Kumarihamis, Maithri and Sunil. Underneath were the words "The Nelum family awaits the case decision ".

Nimal looked at Sunil's photograph with great desire. While thinking of cutting the photograph and pasting it on his suitcase he looked at the heading happily. He saw in large letters, " Nelum Bandara goes to gaol for six months. "

Nimal could not believe his own eyes. It was then that he thought how much more important are words than pictures. For a long time he did not see anything else in the news paper. Just as when eyes are covered with a veil of tears he was not able to see anything. Instantly the clock struck two. With the sound of the clock the bell too rang. That is the time when classes begin. Nimal too traced his steps towards the carpentry classes, thoughtfully.

Chapter Forty Seven

Although Nimal went to the carpentry class his mind was still with Sunil. Yet Nimal born in sorrow and living in sorrow could forget sorrow and do the work that he is doing because he is quite used to it. Therefore the weaving of a chair that was fixed for that day was completed very well within the specified time.

As he was doing the work he told himself something very slowly. It was " There is a solution always for any problem. " This was what the principal always tells the boys.

The problem that Nimal has is Sunil's sorrow. What is the solution for it. Has Sunil completely stopped going to school? Nimal of course can study in a boarding school now.

Nimal went to meet the principal. That was to bring up the question and find out a solution for it. But instead of explaining the reason why he came he kept on looking at the principal with tear filled eyes.

" Why Nimal are you with tear filled eyes? Is it because Sunil's father was sent to jail? "

" Yes " he said with a bow.

Nimal was surprised at the principal saying what Nimal had in his mind.

" All this time Sunil was sad because of Nimal. Now Nimal is sad because of Sunil. Sunil is anxious to get Nimal released and get him back to the village"

The principal went on explaining to Nimal what Nimal knew as well as what Nimal did not know. He told Nimal that he came to know this from Nimal's and Sunil's teacher Miss. Shanthi. Now Miss. Shanthi is principal of Gemunu Vidyalaya. She and the principal had been at the university together revealed the principal further.

" Now Nimal you are released aren't you. Why do you now grieve? " asked the principal.

" Yet as a reason of my boarding house scholarship I am unable to go home, that is the reason " answered Nimal.

" Once you go to a Vidyalaya with a Boarding without trouble you can study and learn. After passing big exams and doing a good profession you can live happily " the principal carefully explained.

" While Sunil, my parents, brothers and sisters are suffering what is the happiness that I have? If I am able to go home I can help them even a little. Now I can do carpentry extremely well. Sunil too will be happy " argued Nimal.

" You learn well, get a good appointment and you can receive a handsome salary isn't that so Nimal"

" I grow big, do a big job and until I earn money they will die away having nothing to eat and drink. Sir, as you say if there is a solution for every question, what is the solution for this one, please tell me " said Nimal.

" Yes if there arises a question there must be a solution. I shall think it over and see. Now it's games time? Forget these and do your work according to the time table "

Obeying the principal's orders Nimal went away

Chapter Forty Eight

Two days passed. No answer whatsoever was received from the principal. On the third morning Nimal received a message. Accordingly Nimal went up to the room of the principal and knocked at the door.

" Who is that? "

" Nimal "

" Please come in "

Nimal went inside the office. He, seeing Sunil and Miss Shanthi seated there watched them as if he had turned to stone. Without his knowledge his arms came together. The eyes became wet.

" Do you know them? " asked the principal.

" Yes " answered Nimal.

A servant came carrying a tray and served them with biscuits and tea. While all four were taking tea the principal addressed them.

" Sunil wants Nimal released and get him to the village. Nimal also wants to go back to the village. But since Nimal has received a scholarship to a boarding school if he accepts the scholarship he will not be able to go to the village because there is no boarding school in the village. Does Sunil like Nimal going to a boarding school to learn and do a big job, or to get him to the village and remain without going to school? " asked the principal in a deep voice.

Sunil remained thoughtful for a little while. All three were looking at him.

" I like Nimal going to a big Vidyalaya more " said Sunil.

Sunil and Miss Shanthi looked at one another and smiled kindly.

" Nimal what do you say? "

" I want to go back home. If I go home I can do a job and be of help to the parents and also stay with Sunil " said Nimal firmly.

The principal addressed Miss Shanthi in order that Sunil and Nimal could hear.

" I discussed this question with the president of the Sri Lanka Samaja Sewa Sangamaya. She and the Executive Body accepted that this should be settled as a human problem. The aim of the Samaja Sewa Sangamaya is that Nimal should be made to live in a good environment and that he should be given a sound education. In order to put this into effect I was given permission to adopt a suitable method for this. I am very happy that Miss Shanthi is willing to take over that responsibility on behalf of Nimal. Even if Gemunu Vidyalaya does not have residential facilities since the Samaja Sewa Sangamaya has undertaken to fulfil its promise I took permission to entrust the scholarship money to Miss Shanthi. Here are the documents in respect of this. " The president handed over to Miss Shanthi the bundle of documents.

Nimal stayed dumbstruck for a while and then dropped at the feet of the principal and worshipped him.

Chapter Forty Nine

At midday someone was seen coming down from the stone quarry. The betel tray kept on Ranmenika's lap was placed on the ridge of the verandah by her and getting on to the courtyard while slicing the arecanut she made a further survey of the place.

" Isn't that Nimal putha who is coming? " she inquired so that her husband too could hear.

Muthu Banda who had broken stones from morning had after coming from the quarry eaten a kurrakkan roti and was resting on the mat in the verandah after closing his eyes. When he heard what his wife had said he got up and walked two or three feet towards the edge of the courtyard and resting his two hands on the hips he stood and looked.

" If you are coming today too after running away you need not come here " said Muthu Banda in an angry voice.

" Stay without making a fuss " said Ranmenika handing the chew of betel to him and standing at the head of the gate so that he was covered by her.

" It's I who have to waste my time going to Police stations. You are not the one " he said reducing his temper and putting the chew of betel into his mouth.

Trying to hide his shyness that arose from the talk of parents by a slight smile, Nimal hopping from one stone to another as he was accustomed stepped down silently and came on to the courtyard.

Muthu Banda seeing Nimal clad in an immaculate white pair of trousers and an immaculate white shirt, wearing a pair of black shoes and carrying an expensive travel bag thought that it was not a runaway journey and did not want to lessen the dignity that he had put on at the start but looked on with the fierce looking face.

" Why in haste? " asked the mother taking the bag into her hand and reducing the heaviness of the mind as well as that of the hand.

" There is no haste " said Nimal, and in the courtyard itself held appachchi's feet as well as his mother's feet and placing his head on them Nimal worshipped them.

Although worshipping Nimal's parents was not a new thing, worshipping them with his head on their feet may be construed as if he was seeking their pardon for having caused himself to be sent to the reformatory. The mother wiped her tears with the edge of the 'Osariya' and the father kept his hand on his head and looking aside suppressed his tears. The three of them became dumb for a moment.

" I was released appachchi " Nimal explained.

" Why when there is time still? " said Muthu Banda putting on a suspicious face and still staring.

" I was given a scholarship, that's the reason "

" What is it ? " asked mother.

" For higher studies in a large boarding school, free "

Ranmenika, not knowing anything looked here and there. Ranmenika who saw that her husband was silent knowing that it could not be bad news looked at the father and the son alternately with a smiling face.

Since Nimal became aware that even appachchi could not clearly understand the matter he gave a letter from his bag to appachchi. In this letter given by the chief of the reformatory all the particulars were found." The principal of Gemunu Vidyalaya Miss Shanthi will come home in the evening and give more particulars " explained Nimal further.

Ranmenika who saw that the husband was relieved more by this realized what happened to her son was solely a great benefit. She smiled faintly and kissed Nimal's head and heaved a sigh. She wiped her eyes with the hem of the ' Osariya ' and went towards the kitchen.

" Then change your clothes will you " said Muthu Banda and taking the letter he sat on the ' pila' and remained there looking at it.

Chapter Fifty

Nimal wore the banian and the checked sarong taken out of his bag. Taking the bag he went in to the kitchen and sat close to the hearth touching the mother who was scraping coconut.

" Your clothes will get dirty son "

" Mother where is sister ? "

" Sister went towards Aluth Walauwa carrying the little sister. She will come in a little while. "

" Maybe to pound rice " he said keeping a little paper bag in mother's hand.

" What's this son? " she asked as if she did not hear about pounding rice.

" Open and see will you "

There was in it a violet coloured piece of poplin cloth.

" That was chosen and given to me by Shanthi Mathiniya, for two jackets for mother and sister. I bought this shirt for appachchi; when appachchi's anger goes down you alone must give it "

" From where is the money , son? "

" The money realized by the sale of the furniture made there is also given to us. I have hundred rupees more money. Here is "

" Yes, no need for us, enough that you came by the grace of the Gods. This cloth may be very expensive isn't it? " Mother shed more tears.

" What is on the hearth? " Nimal changed the conversation.

" Kekulu rice for you "

" I came after eating. At what time does the school close? " he asked and pushed a toffee into her mouth.

" They may be coming now. What's this? "

" Some toffees for brothers and sisters. Give appachchi also " he said and handed a small paper bag to her.

" You, yourself must give when he comes "

Nimal uncovered the coconut leaf wattiya in a corner of the kitchen and looked. There were a few kurakkan rotis and a 'kochchi chilli' sambol on an enamel plate.

" Did you all eat those in the afternoon? "

" Son, what do you eat there in the afternoon? "

" In the afternoon and in the night by turns we eat mutton, fish, two vegetables and rice"

" In the morning? "

" Bread or hoppers or pittu with pol sambol or juggery or jam and milk tea and at about four butter biscuits and milk tea "

" In vain son you came after leaving the place "

" These are more tasty than those mother. Feed me with a piece of roti "

" Wait till kekulu rice is cooked, son "

" Keep the rice for the little ones "

The mother also fed him lovingly with three or four pieces of roti sandwiched with kochchi sambol.